ST JUDE'S CATHEDRAL SCHOOL AND THE OXFORD LEAGUE OF WITCHES

L. M. Guy

Copyright © 2022 L.M. Guy

All rights reserved

The characters and events portrayed in this book are fictitious. Any similarity to real persons, living or dead, is coincidental and not intended by the author.

No part of this book may be reproduced, or stored in a retrieval system, or transmitted in any form or by any means, electronic, mechanical, photocopying, recording, or otherwise, without express written permission of the publisher.

ISBN-13: 9798436314242

Cover design by: Guy & Co

Printed in Great Britain

CONTENTS

Title Page
Copyright
Chapter 1 - What Shall We Ban?   1
Chapter 2 - Tedious and Brief   18
Chapter 3 - Rupert's Dark Past   35
Chapter 4 - Sausages and Spectres   55
Chapter 5 - A Series of Revelations   72
Chapter 6 - The Colosseum and the Clues   91
Chapter 7 - A Visit to the Castle   107
Chapter 8 - The Book of Dreams   126
Chapter 9 - The Ruby in the Sky   147
Chapter 10 - In the Archive   167
Chapter 11 - The League of Witches   187
Chapter 12 - Isolda   208
Chapter 13 - The Witch's Miniature   226
Books By This Author   249

CHAPTER 1 - WHAT SHALL WE BAN?

Mr Mond, the Pastoral Deputy Head of St Jude's, was allegedly registering the pupils as they arrived, whilst Dr Botherby, never content to restrict himself to academic matters, interfered with the administrative affairs. As Mr Mond, despite his many excellent qualities, was frightfully uneducated, this interference of his eminent colleague always made him very uneasy, for though Dr Botherby was quite fussy enough to take his job, he did not feel himself capable of becoming the de facto Head of Academics. Thus, as he ticked the children off his list, the mind of Mr Mond was far from tranquil. Peering from his great height at his more diminutive colleague, he contemplated the manoeuvres he would make against him, causing him to frown rather severely whenever a pupil interrupted his thoughts. This was not owing to any antipathy towards children; unlike many teachers, Mr Mond took pleasure in his occupation during months other than July and August. Rather, he frowned because at every interruption he found himself obliged to begin his thoughts again, and it must be confessed that thinking was not his forte.

Meanwhile, Dr Botherby was engaged in an intricate plan for the academic reform of St Jude's, which involved generally uprooting centuries of tradition. For Dr Botherby was, in spite of his Oxford education, very open minded and innovative. Unfortunately, my Muse finds herself much baffled by the thoughts of this learned educational theorist, being more accustomed to less serious subjects, but she will make an attempt to reveal them to the gracious reader. Briefly, then, Dr Botherby's plan was to eventually abolish sets and have chemistry taught by the physics teacher, and so forth. Now I must confess that it is utterly beyond me to fathom the reasoning behind these reforms, but they undoubtedly stemmed from profound wisdom, for the minds of great men work in mysterious ways, incomprehensible to the ordinary mortal. At any rate, Dr Botherby was acutely aware that he was much ahead of his time and that his genius was woefully misunderstood; therefore, he planned his reforms much as Philip of Spain planned the Armada, that is to say, with no intention of doing anything personally.

Indeed, the Head of Academics had other ambitions. Observing the difficulties which his illustrious colleague occasionally had with the Gordian knot of pastoral affairs in a school like St Jude's, he was quite prepared to do as Alexander did and cut the knot for him. Alas, Mr Mond was quite content with the Gordian knot the way it was and did not quite appreciate the doctor's good intentions in forcibly alleviating some of his duties.

'Mr Mond, has the new biology teacher arrived yet? I desire to communicate with her,' said Dr Botherby slowly and majestically.

While Mr Mond considered this, he pulled his hat further down onto his head and his scarf further up, so that only his owlish eyes, staring anxiously from behind thick glasses, could be properly seen. This made him look very distinguished, notwithstanding the resemblance to a specimen in a glass case at a museum.

Mr Mond, having considered, replied, 'I don't think so. Was there anything particular you wanted to say to her?'

'That is quite immaterial. What is of the essence, is that she should be here,' remarked Dr Botherby severely. 'The unpunctuality of teachers these days is positively reprehensible. Do you concur with me?'

Mr Mond took a moment to digest all those long words and then replied in the affirmative. Dr Botherby was in no way vexed by the slight delay, for he was fond of impressing his colleague by making it both his principle and his practice to use ten words where two would suffice.

'By the by,' he resumed, 'have you written the script yet for the house plays?'

'Indeed I have,' replied Mr Mond rather proudly. 'There are five acts and it is very sensational. However, I'm afraid Mrs Johnson will consider it improper. Not that it is, of course, but you know that she has very strict views. Also, there's a bit of a shortage of adverbs. Do you think it matters very much?'

'I consider that, all things taken into due consideration, the lack of adverbs you mention will not materially hinder the work from giving satisfaction in general,' he replied solemnly.

We shall now leave them to their contemplations and introduce the reader to the juvenile population of St Jude's. The courtyard was bustling with children being dropped off by their parents, who, incidentally, represented a very diverse cross-section of the sort of society one finds at provincial private schools.

'Now, Rupert, remember to telephone us and ensure to take your tablets and wash behind your ears,' admonished the mother of a boy of about fourteen.

'Yes, I will remember, but I'd rather you answered the phone than father: the boys found it a bit peculiar when the dormitory was suddenly filled with him shouting down the phone, and I've had considerable trouble convincing them that my parents are not eccentric,' replied Rupert, smiling.

'I'm not eccentric at all,' protested his father, 'but I am really not accustomed to all this technology. It has ruined my life. After all, it is difficult enough communicating with roofers from deepest Wales in person, let alone on the telephone. At this rate, the guttering on the east wing will never be fixed.'

'Never mind,' said his son comfortingly. 'The guttering on the east wing has been faulty for the last twenty years at least, so I'm sure the Welsh plumber can't do any harm. Well, goodbye Mother, goodbye

Father. I shall see if my friends have arrived yet.'

So saying, he wandered off, whilst the father asked in genuine astonishment, 'My dear, were you aware that Rupert had friends?'

'Indeed, he has informed you of the fact before,' replied his wife. 'Come, let us return to the castle.'

'Extraordinary,' he murmured. 'I wonder if Rupert can understand the plumber's dialect.'

Meanwhile, Rupert had got himself registered and had the customary conversation with Mr Mond, which he had been having every start of term since year seven. It went something like this:

Rupert: Good morning, Mr Mond. How are you?

Mr Mond: Very ill indeed. I suffer a great deal.

Rupert: Well, I'm sorry to hear that, sir.

Mr Mond: Thanks, how are your psychological issues?

Rupert: Better than ever, thank you.

Whereupon Rupert escaped before further inquiry could be made into his psychological issues, which were in fact non-existent, but which Mr Mond was much attached to. Mr Mond was firmly convinced that any child who was the slightest bit abnormal had psychological issues, and none of the children liked to contradict this theory, which would have put him quite out. It may as well be here recorded, that Mr Mond was rather popular despite his peculiarities, for he possessed the great virtue of giving very short assemblies.

'Bertie!' cried Rupert, catching sight of his friend. 'I

say, what have you done to your hair? Are you, by any chance, impersonating a convict?'

This sally was greeted by a gesture of great alarm, accompanied by a furtive glance at the lady of formidable aspect who was escorting poor Bertie. To his distress, it appeared from the expression of his aunt, for such she was, that she had heard and was affronted by the remark. Rupert, realising he had made a grave diplomatic error, looked apologetically at his friend.

'Who is that, Ethel?' asked the aunt severely.

'Aunt Caroline, Aunt Caroline, I am very much attached to my third syllable!' cried Bertie piteously. 'You have just undone two years' painstaking work in living down the unfortunate fact of my having been christened Ethelbert, which is bad enough, but to shorten it to anything other than Bertie is beyond dreadful.'

'Do not fuss, and be so good as to answer my question,' said Aunt Caroline, while Bertie looked beseechingly at Rupert.

'Aunt Caroline, this is my friend Rupert,' he stammered.

Though the aunt was rather shorter than both boys, she appeared to be in all points a formidable woman, so that Bertie, usually very lively, was quite abashed by her severe gaze; although it was not he who had made the unfortunate remark, he stood convicted in his own eyes.

'Madame, I am your humble servant,' said Rupert gallantly, with a charming smile. 'Bertie has told me so much about you, but I did not suppose I should have the honour of meeting you.'

Bertie stared and made a face, indicating his view that his friend had been reading too many French novels over the holidays, but the aunt did not seem to think anything of it. On the contrary, she even condescended to exchange a few commonplace remarks with Rupert before leaving her nephew with much good advice. As he was busy marvelling at how his friend had managed to establish himself in Aunt Caroline's good opinion after such a disastrous beginning, it is doubtful whether he heeded her admonishments.

'Well, that was amazing. I mean to say, she was positively friendly to you,' Bertie remarked admiringly when his aunt had left. 'I always thought Aunt Caroline never forgave anyone who offended her, though that may just apply to family members after all.'

Rupert laughed, 'I have much experience in making myself agreeable to middle-aged ladies. Did you have a nice summer?'

'Yes and no. The first half was splendid, but then Aunt Caroline came to stay with us and told my mother that she was bringing me up all wrong. She hasn't got children, which I suppose makes her an authority on the subject. Anyway, my mother listens to her out of habit,' said Bertie. 'What's more, my hair was getting a bit long, and Mummy didn't get round to cutting it, so she did,' his large brown eyes grew even larger at the thought. 'Is it very dreadful, Rupert?'

Rupert examined him carefully for a moment and pronounced his hair to be only moderately dreadful.

7

This comforted Bertie a little, and when Rupert said that Matron might be able to do something about it out of pity, he became quite cheerful again.

'Apparently we have a new biology teacher. Do you think she's a real one?' asked Bertie.

'Oh yes, for there are enough pushy parents in the school to raise serious objections if she isn't, and Dr Botherby is too anxious about parental opinion to actually carry out his educational theory.'

There was no time for further discussion on the subject, for the whole school was promptly herded into one of the Head's assemblies. Incidentally, she gave the same assembly every year, judiciously assuming that nobody would remember it from the previous year. As she was in many ways a formidable woman, even Mr Mond pretended to pay great attention, though he was in fact engaged in inspecting the new biology teacher.

Miss Gourlay, being both pretty and charming, had made quite an impression on the male teachers and even the severe Dr Botherby, not usually susceptible to such influences, forgave her for being late and arriving at the wrong entrance. Her face was pale, like a pink rose which is almost white, and framed by flowing hair as black as the night. She had a strangely seductive smile, yet it never quite reached her chestnut eyes, which always concealed more than they expressed. Despite all this, she possessed the remarkable ability of remaining liked by other women as well as attracting men, which made her very remarkable indeed, as Mrs Johnson herself expressed approval and decided to take her under her wing. Of course, Mrs Johnson always had the last word in establishing the collective opinion of the staffroom.

Naturally, she was much discussed by the students at break time. Rupert and Bertie had installed themselves on the usual bench outside the music department and were waiting rather impatiently for the girls. At least, Rupert was, for Bertie had become quite anxious about his hair, having been informed in the previous lesson that it was dreadful.

'There you are, Ada, what's kept you so long?' asked Rupert, jumping up.

'It is only three minutes into break,' Ada looked at her watch and smiled, 'but Beatrice and I had to have the customary conversation with Mr Mond.'

'Oh, we managed to have it this morning in the courtyard,' said Rupert.

'Ah, but you two don't have Mrs Johnson as your form tutor. She talked at length, and she's making me sit by a boy who persists in talking about football.'

'I sympathise deeply,' said Rupert, thinking that had he been in the place of said boy, he would have talked about a great many interesting things. 'What do you two think about Miss Gourlay?'

'Well, I haven't actually spoken to her, but I do know she upset Dr Botherby by coming through the castle ruins and in through the back entrance,' replied Beatrice.

'That's one fire already lit, then,' remarked Ada. 'When anyone goes to a new place they have to light three fires before they settle down, and with maternity cover teachers, by the time they've lit them, their time is almost past. So it's a good thing that she's efficient.'

'The Head has lit rather more than three fires,' said Bertie.

'She is quite a different matter,' replied Ada. 'She is very accomplished at revolutionising things, and she is an ardent feminist, therefore, it's only to be expected. I gather from Mr Mond, by the way, that his new play will cause controversy.'

'Last year's certainly did, when the heroine, having tragically died at the end of the first half, somehow managed to get married at the end,' said Rupert.

'Maybe we just need to be more open minded to modern literature,' suggested Ada, 'in which anything's possible.'

'Certainly not! I am extremely closed minded, and a whole regiment of Mrs Johnsons shall not change my opinion that modern literature is either tedious or disturbing,' cried Rupert emphatically. 'I shall die in it at the stake!'

'Mr Mond said that this time his play is sure to be very popular with the boys, but that Mrs Johnson may find it improper. Apparently she had a great deal to say about his incorrect use of semicolons,' said Beatrice gravely.

'I imagine that means it's something in the Don Juan line, hence the controversy,' remarked Ada.

At this juncture, Mr Dodd the choirmaster waddled onto the scene, clearly bursting with news. The children had barely greeted him when he exclaimed with righteous indignation, 'It is dreadful! She can not do it. Even Cromwell would not have done it.'

This was very serious indeed, as, in Mr Dodd's vocabulary, Cromwell was synonymous with disaster.

In answer to the question of what it was which Cromwell would not have done, he cried, 'She has become a Puritan!'

'Well, sir, Cromwell certainly did do that,' Rupert laughed.

'It isn't amusing at all,' said Mr Dodd severely. 'She, that is, the Head has banned all the decent hymns and all the latin bits of the service have to go, and, what's infinitely worse, she's making us sing the new version of 'The Lord's My Shepherd'. It is dreadful!'

'I didn't know there was a new version, but if she's making us sing modern hymns, maybe it's time to leave choristers after all. My voice may break suddenly,' said Rupert significantly.

'What nonsense! You'll never be a bass, anyway,' replied Mr Dodd indignantly.

'I should hope not, Mr Dodd,' said Rupert. 'Only tenors who can't sing in tune become basses.'

'But what am I to do?' asked Mr Dodd.

'You could just ignore the Head's injunctions. I mean, she can't complain till after the service,' suggested Bertie, 'by which time it will be too late.'

Mr Dodd shuddered, 'My constitution won't be able to stand it afterwards though. And to think she was a Chorister herself when she was at school! Anyway, the Cathedral won't like all this reform; they've always been very high church, but the three heads always want to ban things. They will ban music next, and I'll be out of a job, you'll see.'

'Well, Mr Dodd, I think I may have a solution,' said Ada thoughtfully. 'If you were to inform the Head that you agreed with her after all, and then carry out her instructions to an extreme degree, she might change her mind, out of a desire to oppose you. You could always ask for a particularly monotonous sermon, to persuade her a bit.'

'That is brilliant!' cried Mr Dodd, quite happy again. 'I shall begin my campaign at once.'

'Mr Dodd always makes Cathedral matters sound like some sort of battle,' observed Bertie, when he had left.

'Of course, we used to have the Crusades; now we have the Head,' said Rupert. 'The question is, what will they ban next? I mean, they are obliged to ban something.'

Though he spoke partly in jest, Rupert was right, for at that very moment, Mr Mond and Dr Botherby were contemplating this very important question. As it is much easier to ban something than to implement something, the deputy heads of St Jude's were both rather anxious to assert their influence by banning something first. However, Mr Mond's proposition of banning biscuits was roundly rejected by the staffroom, so he was busy thinking.

'I suggest we abolish compulsory Latin up to GCSE and just make it an option,' said Dr Botherby, looking anxiously at Mr Jury, the Latin teacher, over his glasses.

'Yes, I concur with you,' replied Mr Jury, to the general astonishment of the teachers. 'Well, I'd have much better results if only people who were good at Latin took it, and, after all, it's only the results most of the parents care about. We only advertise ourselves as giving a rounded education on paper, but nobody expects it in practice!'

'Mr Jury, you should not say such things,' admonished Mrs Johnson. 'People will be offended.'

'I like to offend people!' cried Mr Jury. 'Anyhow, we must let Dr Botherby abolish something.'

'Indeed, I am gratified by your unexpected enthusiasm, Mr Jury, but we must proceed with caution,' observed Dr Botherby. 'Everything must be done slowly and after careful consideration and deliberation,' he paused impressively for the benefit of Mr Mond, who was looking perplexed. 'For I should greatly regret to offend people, as Mrs. Johnson judiciously observed just now, therefore the utmost discretion and circumspection are required, so that, in the fullness of time, my aim will be accomplished.'

Dr Botherby would have gone on longer, but he ran out of breath, so Mr Jury took the opportunity to insert the words 'carpe diem' into the conversation, and as the learned doctor had forgotten what they meant, he simply pulled up his scarf even further and looked solemn. The audience not appearing sufficiently impressed, he also put on his gloves and hat, and polished his glasses. This worthy teacher, it must be noted, was in his way as great a martyr as St Jude, for he often overheated himself in order to look dignified. Had the saint been alive in the 21st Century, he would certainly have patronised Dr Botherby's cause, which was a great and hopeless one, especially as nobody, except the man himself, was quite sure what the cause was.

The next morning before school, Ada went into the music building, as was her custom. Owing to the zeal of the caretaker, all the piano rooms except room seven were locked. A little disappointed, for the piano in that room was usually more out of tune than the others, she began to play. However, as her fingers ran over the keys, the garish ceiling lights and flaky white paint on the walls vanished. The pedal groaned and made a noise like a duck, the keys were dusty and tired, and somewhere in the distance the sound of a lawnmower intruded on the most beautiful music. But none of it mattered, for she was far away in that paradise which we only enter through dreams and music, and the poor, battered instrument somehow managed to soar passionately with her as if it were young again and had not been pounded by generations of pupils.

She did not hear the soft footsteps approaching, nor did she sense Rupert's presence outside the door. He leaned against the wall and listened, motionless. As he watched her elegant fingers coax the music out of the piano, an enraptured smile lit up his intense, green eyes. It occurred to him in passing that she had a lovely profile; he would have liked to see her in a dress. I hope the reader will excuse this sign of triviality on his part, but my Muse insists on being true to life, and therefore does not allow me to write about a boy who is not superficial.

It would not be accurate, or, I fear, acceptable to the modern reader, to say he loved her at that moment. Boys of fourteen do not fall in love, but Rupert was by nature susceptible and education had rather encouraged this tendency to romanticism than suppressed it. Thus, as the yearning strains of Schumann's Dedication washed over him - she had not yet reached the end, in which Liszt somehow turned it into a virtuoso piece - he felt his heart trembling and palpitating with a strange ecstasy, and he wondered innocently if this were love. Considering for a moment, he decided against it, for his reading of Byron, Shelley, Heine etc. had left him with the strong impression that all lovers are doomed to misery, whereas he was very happy indeed. He wanted the moment to last forever, for him to listen eternally. Incidentally, had she turned round at that point and seen him with his glowing eyes and cheeks, which were usually too pale, flushed delicately, she would have thought him very handsome; at any rate, she did not, and it did not occur to her to look at him closely at this or any other time.

Suddenly, she heard the piano in the next room surging in unison with her, and an ethereal voice singing. Enchanted, she stopped and listened, but she thought it very curious, for she was quite sure that the room was locked. Ada looked at the monotonously ticking clock: it was five minutes to eight. Usually, the caretaker only came to open the music rooms at eight, if he had locked them the previous night. Besides, there was a mesmerising quality about that airy voice which seemed so out of place in the dull music department of St Jude's.

Rupert heard the voice too. A tremor ran through him, and his eyes opened very wide. Peering into room eight, he waved his hand as if in greeting, and was about to say something, when Ada came out. They both looked through the glass. He appeared agitated and tried to direct her attention elsewhere. Then he sighed as he realised that she too had seen the keys of the piano going down, but nobody playing.

'Rupert, there's nobody here, yet I know I heard the music,' she said, bewildered.

'Yes, me too,' he replied. 'Oh dear, is that the time? We must hurry to the refectory, or there won't be any breakfast left.'

So saying, he rushed her out of the music department, wondering to himself how on earth he would explain to her what they had both seen but only he had understood.

'You always play Schumann beautifully; I was quite enraptured,' he said shyly.

'Thanks,' she smiled, feeling shy too all of a sudden.

When the four children met at break time, they found a sign on the door, written by the caretaker in large, clumsy letters: *Pupils are Not Allowed in the music department out of school hours and Ghosts are Not Allowed At All.* This sign caused great amusement to the children, but the staff were rather displeased. Mrs Johnson thought that it was not politically correct to discriminate against supernatural beings, considering the unusual number of them at school, and Mr Mond and Dr Botherby were upset that the caretaker had banned something first.

CHAPTER 2 - TEDIOUS AND BRIEF

After lessons that day, Mr Mond's sensational play was at last unveiled to the world, and each house hastened to begin their rehearsals. As with all preparations for house events, these were extremely chaotic, and involved much ado about nothing, so that everybody was quite satisfied at the end of them.

'What-ho, Ernest!' called Rupert. 'How are you managing with the organisation? Not very well, I imagine, for you don't seem to have anyone to organise you.'

'Thank heavens you're here,' cried Ernest. 'I do wish your classmates - I presume they are not your friends - would be quiet momentarily so I can make some sense of this script, but I don't suppose it will ever happen. Oh dear, I appear to have lost the fourth page, or rather, someone's purloined it.'

While he fumbles around for the missing page, we shall draw his portrait in a few strokes for the reader. He was seventeen years old, tall, handsome and well dressed - for a sixth former in a second rate private school, let it be understood, meaning that his blazer was only moderately ill-fitting and his shirt and tie were not lurid. He was considered to be rather clever and had a vast fund of anecdotes from the times of Romulus till last Tuesday; he could generally be relied upon to predict exam questions with reasonable accuracy and would good-naturedly rattle through an answer if requested. However, this did not help his popularity as much as may be expected, for, as is often the case, those asking the questions rarely understood the answers. Like many such boys, he was deeply attracted to the female of the species in general, in a poetic, abstract fashion, and had a great horror of small children and fuss. Thanks to these fundamentally conflicting sentiments, Ernest was remarkably immune to the charms of the girls in his year, who were both fussy and prosaic.

'Indeed, page four is very necessary to the script, and it's no use to me as a paper aeroplane,' Ernest complained. 'You are informing me that it's been launched out of the window?' The small child thus addressed nodded gravely. 'I say, this is getting a bit thick. Well, everything is for the best, as Dr Pangloss, and occasionally Dr Botherby says, for at least I will not be tormented by Mr Mond's grammar on that page.'

'What's the play about?' asked Bertie.

'That, my dear Bertie, is what I am trying to deduce,' he replied. 'It appears to be a womanising sort of play. There's a fair amount of duelling and women fainting. Oh, and there's a lady who goes mad in act two, which is always interesting. Yet what the play is actually about is a bit of a mystery: there are so many apparently unrelated incidents, as if Mr Mond just inserted as many sensational elements as possible without worrying about plot at all.'

'It sounds very innovative and original,' observed Rupert, 'and modern.'

The other two boys laughed, for these words all meant dreadful, in Rupert's vocabulary.

'Precisely!' cried Ernest. 'However, on the positive side, almost everybody dies at the end; happy endings always make me feel quite miserable.'

'He has missed the meaning of fiction, in that case,' said Rupert. 'The good end happily and the bad, unhappily, you know. If only he had written it like that, he could have pretended it was moral, and Mrs Johnson wouldn't disapprove.'

'Ah, but there are no good and bad characters, only ridiculous and more ridiculous,' replied Ernest. 'Well, Mr Jury did tell me to wait for him to get more copies of the script, but he isn't here, so I might just start without him. It won't make much difference anyway, for I'm planning on using much artistic licence with the lines. Wish me luck, chaps, for I'll need it.'

Rupert and Bertie wished him luck in a tone which implied that they did not think it would do much good. Ernest stared for a moment at the crowd of noisy children quarrelling and shrieking, and it seemed to him like a turbulent sea in which he was about to drown himself. However, he reflected that if he were to make himself ridiculous, now was the time to do it, before Mrs Johnson or some other formidable female teacher came to inspect the rehearsal.

He took a deep breath and began brightly, 'Hello, everyone, welcome to our first rehearsal of Mr Mond's new play, entitled, rather enigmatically, *The Way We Love Nowadays*.'

'Entitled what?' asked one girl in year seven peevishly.

'The way we love nowadays,' repeated Ernest.

'Yes, yes, I know what the title is, but what did you say before that?'

'I just said that it was enigmatically entitled. You know what enigmatically means, I presume,' he replied, slightly exasperated.

'I don't, and you should not use such long words which nobody understands,' she admonished severely.

This remark disconcerted Ernest somewhat, for it had never occurred to him that he used overly long words, and the prospect of having his speech censored all term was not a pleasant one. He felt much as Gulliver did among the Yahoos, as he reflected that directing Mr Mond's play would be more difficult than he had anticipated, owing to the fact that he would have to direct people as well as words.

'Well, I'm sure you understand me, don't you, Rupert?' Ernest looked appealingly at his younger friend.

'Certainly,' said Rupert.

'Only because he's a nerd like you,' observed the girl.

'Ah, Ernest,' whispered Rupert, 'can you explain to

me what exactly a nerd is?'

'It is a derogatory term for an academically accomplished individual, stereotypically, but not always, wearing ridiculous glasses and being socially awkward.'

'Oh, I see,' said Rupert. 'I'm glad I don't wear glasses. Do proceed with what you were going to say.'

'Right-ho,' said Ernest. 'Yes, as I was saying, it is an unusual title for the play, considering there is no love, only a great deal of courting and that it is certainly not set nowadays. I did think it was in the Middle Ages, until the bit with the steam train, but no matter. Also some of the characters managed to die before they were born. However, please don't be discouraged by these discrepancies, which I'm sure we can sort out later; we must simply be open minded and think laterally; we must look for what Mr Mond wanted to say, rather than what he did say. Oh, hello, Mr Jury.'

'Salvete!' though slightly out of breath, the Latin teacher greeted them enthusiastically. 'Sorry I'm late: I had a disagreement with the photocopier.'

'Did you check it was turned on?' asked Ernest.

'Eventually, yes,' said Mr Jury. 'Well, here are enough scripts to go round. You appear distressed.'

'Distressed? Well, I suppose I am a little put out. You see, sir,' Ernest said confidentially, 'objections were made to my manner of talking. I'm not touchy about it, you know, but it disconcerted me temporarily. I have an unpleasant presentiment that a fairly considerable proportion of the Lilliputians are not going to take me very seriously.'

'Nil desperandum, my boy,' Mr Jury reassured him cheerfully. 'I think you're doing splendidly.'

'Thanks awfully, Mr Jury. Well, I think we should just start reading through the first act. Can you be the first and second ladies, you two their respective husbands, you the page, Rupert, and you the jester, Bertie? We can change the casting later if it's not working, but I am adhering to the principle of everyone doing what they are good at, providing it is their turn,' explained Ernest. 'Also, can I have a couple of year sevens to be footmen; now I don't mean to be sexist, but footmen ought to be male. Really, I'm very open minded, but I'm going to insist on male footmen. Right, can I have two maids, whom I insist shall be female, please? Just stand at the back and pretend to be setting up a banquet. It says here that the maids are flirting with the footmen, but you have to do it silently and unobtrusively.' One of the footmen made a complaining sound, and Ernest looked up, 'Good heavens! Nowhere in the script does it say that one of the maids must hit the footman on the head, therefore I implore you to refrain from doing so. Thankfully, we now come to a character with a name, though I would never call someone who's meant to be a romantic hero Jeremy.'

The first scene unfolded rather confusingly, for the errant knight Sir Jeremy began courting one lady and ended up courting the second.

'Ernest, I think that's a mistake. Shouldn't I just stick with the one lady?'

'Not necessarily,' said Ernest solemnly. 'Don Giovanni managed to court one thousand and three

Spanish ladies successively, so I don't see why you can't manage two. In all seriousness, though, I think it's meant to be like that so that the lines are evenly distributed. Do carry on, and by the way, the two husbands shouldn't be listening while their wives are being seduced.'

The rehearsal was resumed, but the husbands, not quite sure what to do with themselves, got rather in the way.

'Sorry to interrupt again,' said Ernest, 'but "aside" does not mean walk to the side of the stage. It just means only the page can hear you. Oh look, is that the time? What a pity, we shall have to stop here, so that we can get to prep on time,' Ernest sounded very relieved. 'Next rehearsal at the same time tomorrow, please.'

'A slight problem has arisen: the assembly hall has been booked for dance classes tomorrow, and Mrs Johnson will not give up the theatre,' said Mr Jury.

'That's fine, we'll use the sports hall,' said Ernest.

'It's not available either.'

'The courtyard?'

'Mr Mond has installed table tennis there.'

'Mr Jury, we must have a rehearsal tomorrow, even if we have it in the chapel!' cried Ernest.

'There's evensong in the chapel tomorrow,' said Rupert.

'Bother!' said Ernest. 'Very well, we shall rehearse the day after tomorrow,' he added, trying to sound dignified. 'See you all then. Oh, what a mess I have made already!' he sighed to himself.

After prep, the children gathered for dinner, where the conversation mainly concerned Mr Mond's play.

'Our rehearsal went tolerably well,' said Ada, putting her tray down, 'but Mrs Johnson has abridged the play so that it's considerably shorter.'

'Indeed? What for?' asked Rupert.

'To remove the inappropriate parts,' she explained.

'Mrs Johnson feels that it might have a corrupting influence on the minds of young children,' added Beatrice.

'I really think her concerns are superfluous,' said Rupert. 'First, it's not very inappropriate compared to some books in the library.'

'Only the ones in the restricted section,' put in Bertie.

'Secondly,' continued Rupert, 'Mr Mond is far too cunning to be understood, so it will go over their heads anyway, and thirdly, the minds of this year's year sevens are already sufficiently evil for immoral plays not to make the slightest difference.'

'Spoken like the oracle, as usual, Rupert,' chimed in Ernest. 'Can I sit with you? Thanks, I can relax now, at last. All the way through prep, one of the girls was making eyes at me, which isn't the sort of thing a chap wants when he's trying to do questions invented by Mr Beanacre.'

'Making eyes at you?' Rupert was perplexed.

'Well, it's a little hard to explain, and I won't demonstrate,' said Ernest.

'You know, Rupert, it's what frivolous girls do when they wish to intimate to a boy that they find him attractive,' said Ada. 'They usually flutter their eyelashes.'

'Oh, I see. I do know, but I thought it was hay fever.'

'You have a wonderful way of explaining things,' laughed Ernest. 'Perhaps you can explain to me the reason why Mr Mond didn't give the majority of his characters any names in the cast list, even though he thinks of quite a few over the course of the play.'

'Either he thought of the names after and couldn't be bothered to write them in, or he is imitating Dürrenmatt,' said Ada.

'Is that a maker of very hard-wearing carpets?'

'Don't be silly, Ernest. He's a Swiss playwright, whom you are not expected to have heard of, by the way, but the reason I mention him is, that he wrote a play called "Der Besuch der Alten Dame." In this play, hardly any of the characters have names, the point being to alienate the audience, so that they think about what he's trying to say, rather than being distracted by any emotional attachment to the characters. Maybe that's Mr Mond's idea too.'

'Well, he's certainly succeeded in alienating me, but I don't know what he's trying to say, so I'm afraid it rather defeated the object,' said Ernest. 'By the way, have any of you ever been taught by Mr Beanacre?'

'No, but we have him tomorrow for physics. What's he like?'

'Well, you can form your own opinion tomorrow, but I'll just tell you that he once informed my year ten triple science class that an ion is the same as an atom and that Dr Botherby agreed with him on the point, "so don't allow any chemistry teachers to deceive you about it, boys and girls",' Ernest imitated the deep, growly voice of Mr Beanacre and almost choked on his apple crumble.

As the rest of the conversation flitted over sundry trivial matters which are only of interest to those whom they concern, we shall forbear to inflict it on the reader. Indeed, I have no intention of giving the impression that the life of an English private school is fulfilling; the gracious reader, having consulted the books of memory, may find that it chiefly involves fussing. On the other hand, with the gentle trickling by of the years, the fussy parts may have faded away, selectively forgotten, just as the author of the present chronicle has tastefully omitted to tell of the mundane, the unpleasant and the vulgar aspects of school life. Though this paragraph should perhaps have come at the beginning in order to set the anxious mothers of young ladies at ease over the propriety of what follows, I adhere to the maxim, much relied upon by musicians, that late is better than never.

However, that is enough talk: alas, the modern reader has so little patience for loquacious writers who would show them most innocently the book, even of their most secret soul. Therefore let us pass to Old School House, where the children are falling asleep, or rather, where they are supposed to be falling asleep. The dormitories rustled with whispered conversations; the sedate footsteps of Matron faded away. Gradually, as the veil of night was drawn over St Jude's, all fell silent.

Ada lay awake for some time, contemplating. The ethereal voice of the invisible pianist haunted her. She felt a strange affinity to it, as if she had known it all her life. Yet she was preoccupied, for she could not explain it. Could she really have seen the piano playing itself? It was almost like the beginning of a fairytale, but of course she was far too old to believe in the supernatural. For a moment, she was alarmed and she wondered if she really were developing psychological issues, as Mr Mond had predicted so often. After all, she was hearing voices in her head.

However, this thought was only fleeting, for she was quite convinced the voice was real. Rupert had heard it too and seen the keys moving. He had been distracted, preoccupied every time he passed room eight, almost as if he knew something. He had tried very hard to make her forget the incident, but this only increased her impression of it, though she did not speak of it. Whenever they were together, they both sensed the influence of the mysterious voice. Not when there were other people there, but if they were alone, they would look at each other, and then they both knew.

It had not occurred to her until now, that Rupert was not like other people. From the moment they had met, there had been a bond between them. Ostracised by the female cliques, not for any particular reason other than her ignorance of whatever it is they talk about, she took great pleasure in his society, and forgot all the girl dramas when she was with him. They talked about books, music and art, but even when they talked of nothing, there was a fascination in just being with him. Of course, she was vaguely conscious of his admiring her - the rest of year nine had already labelled him her sweetheart, though this was far from the case - but he was so different, so much more refined than the boys who fancied her briefly then grew bored.

However, now that she thought about it, it seemed that there was something mysterious about her friend. He never spoke about his family; it was as if he had no life outside of the school. She was under the impression that he lived in a large house with leaks in the middle of nowhere, but he was so secretive that nobody knew what he did between Friday night and Monday morning. And then, sometimes he knew about things before anyone else did, which was rather strange.

All of a sudden, she felt very tired and seemed to fall asleep imperceptibly. She was not aware of closing her eyes, but a few moments later she found herself in the courtyard, and it was morning. Even as she dreamed, she knew that she was dreaming, but it all seemed so vivid, so real. None of the children walking back and forth were familiar to her, but then she heard a voice which made her shiver.

It was the voice from the music building! The girl was talking to someone whom Ada could not see. Their conversation was of indifferent matters, but she felt mysteriously drawn to her.

'Come on, Margaret,' said the other after a while, and the two girls wandered off.

That other voice seemed vaguely familiar too, as if she had heard it quite recently. She could see Margaret quite clearly, but strangely, her friend was always in the shadow, though the day was bright. Intrigued, she hastened to follow them, so quickly that she collided with a boy rushing in the other direction. However, he carried straight on without noticing it at all. Then she realised that she was only an observer in this scene, that for these people she did not exist, and all of this seemed quite natural to her.

She looked around to see where Margaret had got to, but the next moment, the scene had vanished and she woke up, startled and dizzy.

The next morning, she was perplexed and distracted. Indeed, she was so preoccupied that she did not register Mr Mond asking what she thought of his play, and when she had understood the question, her mind was quite blank as she thought of an answer.

Fortunately, Rupert came to her rescue, remarking very politely, but with a hint of a smile, 'We all thought that your play was very remarkable, sir. I was just saying to myself that you would be known to posterity as the 21st Century's Peter Quince.'

This remark gratified Mr Mond greatly, even more so considering that he was not quite sure what it meant.

'Whatever did you mean by that?' asked Bertie as the children walked to physics.

'That his play is tedious and brief, merry and sad, like Peter Quince's lamentable comedy,' replied Rupert, and the hint of a smile blossomed into a full one.

'The question of course is this: is it a comedy or a tragedy?'

'Comedy, of course,' said Bertie. 'You could never be sad about all those ridiculous characters dying.'

'I thought it was a tragedy,' said Beatrice, 'for it is so badly written that it is quite tragic.'

'What do you think, Ada?' asked Rupert.

'Oh, I disagree with everybody, something which is happening to me with alarming frequency these days.'

'Well, it's either a comedy or a tragedy, isn't it?' asked Bertie.

'No, it is too pathetic for the one and too funny for the other, therefore, I conclude that it is a history play,' said Ada gravely. 'It is the history of Mr Mond's imaginary life.'

The other three agreed, but then a hush descended over all the children as Mr Beanacre poked his head round the door and the class filed in. Mr Beanacre had something of a reputation for irascibility and eccentricity, so that the class was unusually silent. It was in fact so silent, that the insistent ticking of no fewer than seven clocks, which were not quite synchronised, sounded like the galloping of the horses on the day of judgement, whilst the physics teacher himself stared down, seeming to make a judgement on each pupil.

He was rather above average height, although he stooped, which did not prevent him from looking very imposing when he stood still. However, this rarely happened, for he was eternally twitching and fiddling and hopping up and down on his toes. He also had an erratic manner of walking, and when he spoke, his sentences were often fragmented and incoherent; he expressed himself with his hands, eyebrows and facial muscles quite as much as with his mouth. This could have been due to an acute sensibility to the fact that his mouth was unfortunately a little too small for his tongue, a misfortune which he shared with King James I, if the historians are to be believed. However, being only a physics teacher, he was more sensitive about his affliction than the king was about his.

Having imperiously and rather superfluously ordered the class to be silent, he proceeded to have a disagreement with the electronic whiteboard. When Bertie ventured to point out that it would not work until he had turned the computer on, he turned round abruptly and glared, so that poor Bertie became quite confused.

'Don't be silly, Ethelbert, I know what to do!' he cried indignantly.

'Yes,' agreed Bertie hastily. 'Could you please call me Bertie?' he asked timidly. 'All the other teachers call me Bertie, you know, and for the sake of consistency, I was rather hoping you would too.'

Haughtily ignoring this remark, Mr Beanacre admonished the class, who all nodded gravely, 'I told you that it would not work unless the computer was turned on.'

And the lesson progressed. It soon became apparent that he was rather inept, for he kept making mistakes on his own questions. However, nobody quite liked to point this out, so the mistakes remained.

Every time a mistake appeared, the four friends looked at each other from the remote parts of the classroom with increasing anxiety, and Rupert made a tally on the back of the worksheet. By about halfway through, there were eight little pencil marks, and his eyes had gone from expressing amusement to shock and disbelief. Obliviously, Mr Beanacre had ploughed through the lesson like an enraged bull, scattering fragments of physics right and left, and trampling on any which proved obnoxious.

'The acetate rod and the cloth are rubbed together, and electrons are transferred from one to the other,' cried Mr Beanacre vindictively, as though he had a personal grudge against the electrons.

'Which one transfers the electrons, sir? asked one child innocently.

'That is immaterial,' said Mr Beanacre, who did not know, and glared severely at the unfortunate pupil. 'How many r's are in transferred?' he muttered to himself as he wrote on the board.

'Three, but he's only written two.'

'Well, I'm not going to tell him and get my nose bitten off.'

'Someone should tell him. You tell him.'

'I'm scared to point it out. Rupert can tell him.'

These whispers ran round the class like a winter wind, and the general consensus was that Rupert should tell him. Although he was considered a little odd, the other boys usually accepted his views on academic matters as the oracle. The boys on his left and right nudged him significantly, and he smiled an almost sinister smile, before arranging his facial features to express a conscientious interest in the lesson.

What happened next was rather extraordinary, and the entire class stared wonderingly, as the pen picked itself up and wrote on the board. There was nothing so very strange about this, since Mr Beanacre's hand was vaguely attached to the pen, but what shocked everybody was that it seemed to write of its own accord, sweeping Mr Beanacre along with it. Besides, the word 'transferred' was now spelled correctly, which was far from the strangest thing about the incident.

As it happened quite quickly, the children assumed it had merely been a trick of the light. However, Mr Beanacre seemed rather put out and glared at Rupert, he being seated directly in front of him. At that moment, Rupert appeared the picture of innocence: his wide, green eyes were as mild as a still lake and only expressed astonishment that he could be the object of anyone's displeasure. For a second, Mr Beanacre scrutinised him, and he scrutinised Mr Beanacre from behind the mask of apathy which he knew so well how to assume. Although Mr Beanacre proceeded with the rest of his lesson without any change, Rupert occasionally glanced at him with a curious expression in his eyes, as though a veil had been lifted and he was seeing him clearly for the first time.

CHAPTER 3 - RUPERT'S DARK PAST

It is generally acknowledged that most men have a dark past, to some extent. Young ladies are apt to look askance at a man with a stainless reputation as being tedious, just as the rose without a kink or fold in its petals is less beautiful than an imperfect one. Older ladies, on the other hand, have a terrible habit of cynicism, believing firmly that the past of a man which appears pure must be the darkest of all. Anyhow, that is quite enough of philosophy. What I wish to reassure my female readers about, is that Rupert also had a dark past. To be sure, he was only fourteen, but he had always been a rather precocious child, so it follows quite naturally that he should have been ahead of his age in this as well as other things.

At the end of the week, he met his parents by the cathedral, and then disappeared completely, only to re-emerge at a gloomy castle in Wales mainly populated by sheep. The weather, as usual in this part of the world, was somewhat dreary. Shrouded in rain and mist, the crumbled battlements loomed over the hills, on which a few disgruntled sheep resembled small white patches on the landscape.

The drawbridge was lowered with a plaintive creak, and the door was opened by a slightly shrivelled butler. The butler was not particularly old, or at least it was hard to tell his age, but he seemed noticeably withered when observed next to Rupert's mother. If it were not for the presence of a fourteen-year-old son, she could have passed for twenty-five. This was partly because she had a perfect complexion and was very elegant; it was also partly because she was a vampire.

'Welcome back, Madame,' said the butler, smiling graciously and revealing fangs in the process.

It must be noted that in vampire society, it is usually the wives who are in charge: after a few centuries of marriage, the husbands sensibly decide to be under the thumb.

'Did you enjoy school, milord?' the butler looked at Rupert a little disapprovingly, and shook his head.

'Yes, thanks, it was absolutely first class, except for the fact that my physics teacher is a chump,' replied Rupert cheerfully. 'Now, there's no need to look like that. "Chump" is a perfectly legitimate word, it's just that it wasn't invented in the 16th Century.'

'Well, that's only to be expected at St Jude's; I always thought it was second rate,' observed Rupert's father, gazing dreamily into the flickering candle light, as he sank into an armchair (contrary to what many people think, vampire houses are by no means uncomfortable).

'The school is very progressive, at any rate,' smiled

Rupert, 'but Mr Beanacre makes me feel uneasy, and not just because he doesn't know the difference between atoms and ions.'

'Rupert, nor do I, and I hope you are not casting aspersion on my intelligence,' remarked a voice emanating from behind him.

'Not at all, only on your education,' replied Rupert, turning to look at the portrait.

Both Rupert and the portrait grinned, showing their fangs, and the family resemblance suddenly became apparent.

'Anyway, Mother,' he continued, 'there is a strangely sinister air about Mr Beanacre; he is not at all like normal people.' Rupert frowned slightly.

'Well, nor are you,' put in his father.

'I do try ever so hard, but the other boys, apart from Bertie, of course, never see me as one of them,' agreed Rupert a little disconsolately. 'Papa, it is not amusing at all. I can't imagine you were any less socially excluded than I am, but you've just forgotten about it, that's all.'

'There, there, my dear,' said his mother. 'Never pay too much attention to the views of your father. As for your physics teacher, he is probably not of the human species, which is why you can feel a different sort of energy emanating from him.'

'Mr Beanacre is not a human?' Rupert repeated, surprised.

'It's not so very extraordinary,' she replied. 'After all, we have integrated with the humans, and so, for the most part, have the witches, the werewolves and all the other species who resemble humans but have supernatural abilities. They tend to cluster around private schools, presumably because these institutions are so full of eccentric people that they are very inconspicuous, whereas in the state sector they would be noticed at once. Of course, it is not of very much consequence now that there is peace between us all, but the government naturally prefers it if ordinary humans don't know about us: people can be so prejudiced.'

'But Mama, a dreadful thing has occurred. I have been a little foolish,' said Rupert, distressed. 'You see, Mr Beanacre was making ever so many mistakes, and nobody liked to point it out because he is somewhat formidable, and, well, I made the pen write by itself, just for fun and because the boys wanted me to correct him. He didn't say anything, but he glared at me in a rather disconcerting fashion, and I've just realised it's because he knows!'

She laughed at him, 'Really, Rupert, you do take everything so seriously. It doesn't matter that he knows: you have hardly committed a crime.'

'No, that's not the point. He knows I'm a vampire,' he replied. 'And it is more important than you may think. Maybe when I'm grown up I shan't care so much for other people's opinions, but, without being sensitive, the way he looked at me when it dawned on him was as if it were a great sin to be what I am.'

'My dear Rupert,' said his mother tenderly, 'I do understand that it is hard sometimes to be different, but your friends will always like you for yourself. Anyhow, it doesn't matter that Mr Beanacre knows, for so do the Head, Mr Mond and Mrs Johnson.'

'Oh, no wonder Mr Mond keeps asking me if I have psychological issues. And that also explains why Mrs Johnson kept advising me to eat black pudding when I was in her form,' laughed Rupert.

Changing the subject, he entertained his parents with Mr Mond's play.

'Rupert,' said his father gravely, having skimmed through the script, 'this play is utter nonsense! There aren't two lines in it together without a fault, and he is slightly indecent without being amusing, soppy without romance, ridiculous without humour and occasionally serious by accident and without purpose. I'm astounded that you can be willing to act in it; it is not becoming to the family dignity. Isn't that so?' he turned to the portrait.

'Rupert informs me,' replied the latter, 'that acting is no longer considered a disreputable profession, and it would appear that Mr Mond is a great writer of the 21st Century. For, again quoting Rupert, the Muses have left it very barren so far.'

'Well, if that's the case, and Mother approves, I'd better submit at once. We must always listen to the ladies, mustn't we, Rupert? By the by,' he added significantly, 'is there not a certain young lady of whom you are very much enamoured?'

'Certainly not! I mean, I'm awfully fond of Ada, but only platonically,' cried Rupert, turning crimson and lowering his eyes. 'You mustn't tease me, Father, she's nothing to me but a dear friend.'

'Quite so,' he replied, 'but you are rather indifferent to all the daughters of other noble families. The mothers have remarked upon it.'

'Father, I don't like it when they massacre piano sonatas, sing out of tune and with no musicality, quote poetry that they don't understand or even enjoy, and generally exert themselves to appear cultured when really they have nothing at all in their graceful heads,' remarked Rupert a little petulantly.

His father chuckled, 'I hope you haven't allowed the mothers to see your thoughts. Society does not encourage you to have too strong opinions on such matters. You will get a reputation for being a bookworm, which is not quite desirable at your age.'

'The term currently au courant for bookworm is nerd.'

'I shall not use that term: it sounds rather vulgar,' his father replied haughtily. 'The boys don't apply it to you, do they?'

'No,' laughed Rupert. 'The defining characteristics of the nerd are, so I am informed by Ernest, extreme social awkwardness and the wearing of spectacles. As I don't wear glasses, I do not come under this category. For that matter, neither does Ernest, although an obnoxious year seven child informed him that he was a nerd, so maybe the definition isn't too precise.'

'Whether you wear spectacles or not, you shall not be classified as a nerd,' he said gravely.

'Indeed, I'm not very socially awkward after all. Apparently I'm quite in favour with the girls who are not in my classes, mainly because I have never had a conversation of any substance with them,' Rupert sighed languidly, then added in mock despair, leaning his cheek against his hand, 'Girls always start by fancying me; then they despise me; they rarely forgive me. Bertie thinks that I might be able to keep them in the first stage if I don't speak, but I must confess that I'm very fond of talking, so his hypothesis will never be tested.'

'Rupert, my dear, go and get changed for dinner,' broke in his mother. 'We have guests, and they are very traditional. Therefore, let us have none of your school anecdotes, please: as amusing as they are, they are not quite the right thing for this particular audience. If possible, refrain from using any 21st Century vernacular, and avoid at all costs any mention of Mr Mond or Dr Botherby, which would rather shock them.'

'Ok, Mother,' said Rupert, grinning. 'Don't distress yourself, for I'll be positively fascinating. Who are these guests? Here for pleasure or fulfilling social obligations?'

'My dear, it is not good taste to imply that the fulfilling of social obligations is not pleasant,' admonished his mother gently. 'Lady Honoria is an old friend of mine. She will be bringing her daughter, whom I am entrusting to your care. Naturally, his lordship is hardly material. He will be content with a good supply of Bordeaux.'

'I see. Will any transubstantiation take place?'

'I'm afraid I don't understand you.'

'It means turning wine into blood. It's what Catholics do in the Eucharist, though of course, it doesn't really work. I'm not a Catholic, by the by: Mr Dodd wouldn't like that sort of thing in the choir,' laughed Rupert. 'What's the girl like, then?'

'Very proper, mostly silent and mildly disapproving of boys in general, I should imagine, knowing her mother.'

'Wonderful!' he said sarcastically. 'Don't worry, Mama, you'll have no reason to be ashamed of me,' he added, looking back with the whimsical smile peculiar to him, before going to change as instructed.

Rupert climbed the winding staircase to his room pensively. Everywhere the echoes of the past seemed to resound mournfully. The candles flickered and danced, their flames throwing out a fragile light into the dark corners. Usually the castle seemed homely to him, but now the mystery of past centuries clung to the walls, crumbling in places, but still grand. He thought of the ghost at the school and wondered what ghosts and memories may be lurking here, and in the bustling town around the Cathedral of St Jude.

Swapping his white shirt and school tie for the costume of a gentleman in the 16th Century, he inspected himself in the mirror. The tarnished gold figures around the frame stared back mockingly. As he brushed his dark wavy hair, he felt himself caught between two worlds.

Whether in school uniform being the model student or in doublet and hose being the well-trained heir of an old vampire family, he was a little out of place, not quite belonging to either world. That of the present, bustling with traffic and noise, appeared mundane and colourless. That of the past, still very much the present in vampire society, despite superficial appearances of social integration, seemed quaint and almost comical after a week at school. And now the two worlds were colliding; with the ghost of the girl with the beautiful voice haunting him, he felt he was not the same person who had arrived at St Jude's with lively anticipation at the beginning of the week.

For the last time, he studied his reflection. The deep green eyes stared back, gravely, almost sullenly. He wondered idly if he always looked like that.

'Perhaps,' he thought to himself, 'this is the effect of the teenage stage, making me look so melancholy. I'm not a bit melancholy, really. Well, how shall I look tonight? Serious and sensible for Lady Honoria: I shall make very few utterances to her, but I shall nod gravely and wisely to everything she says. To her husband I shall be friendly but not overly lively and talk about horses, for I feel instinctively that he will be the sort of chap who likes talking about horses. As for the young lady, I may be in for a tedious evening if she is already like her mother, which she will be one day with the inevitability of Greek tragedy. In which case she is probably a murderer of music who can't dance, so I shall have to execute a polonaise by myself, or perhaps with a cushion!'

Having tried out his various facial expressions, he galloped gaily down the stairs, until a cough from the butler reminded him to behave with the necessary decorum. A few minutes later, the guests were announced, and Rupert decided that the solitary polonaise might not be called for after all, since the girl was rather pretty.

'My dear, it is so lovely to see you again. I cannot quite remember the last time we had the pleasure of your company, Madeleine,' Lady Honoria smiled at Rupert's mother.

'Last century, I think,' put in his father, bowing. 'Before Rupert was born, at any rate.'

Ignoring this slightly awkward interruption, she replied graciously in kind and admonished her husband with a look.

'Madeleine, your son appears to take after his father, who was such a handsome young man,' continued Lady Honoria with the most affable condescension. 'Fortunately, Rosaline does not resemble hers in the slightest.'

'She seems to be implying I'm not handsome any more. I am somewhat affronted,' he whispered to his son.

Rupert merely nodded and touched the graceful hand proffered to him by Rosaline delicately with his lips. Standing up, he looked into her lustrous eyes for a moment and smiled very politely, but whereas the smile was for the benefit of the parents, the look seemed to be for her alone. A blush mantled her pale cheeks and she rewarded him with a suggestive smile, which they both knew meant nothing in particular, but which made his heart flutter anyway.

Amused, his father secretly made a face at him, which Rupert rather haughtily ignored. The father sighed, realising that the days of making fun of their social circle together would soon be over, as Rupert began paying attention to ladies. This was all very well for him, but his father thought that this was not quite the right time to begin, mainly because he felt in need of moral support when taking the formidable Lady Honoria down to dinner. The moral support was not forthcoming, however, as Rupert and Rosaline were already engaged in an animated discussion about Italian opera. Meanwhile, Lady Honoria had prodded her husband into a state of sufficient consciousness to rouse himself and offer his arm to Rupert's mother before relapsing into good-humoured apathy. She majestically took hold of Rupert's father, and, this swapping of husbands deftly accomplished, sailed into the great hall like a fine ship towing a small rowing boat behind it. He cast his son a piteous look, and then realised that Rupert did not even notice him, being much too occupied talking to the fair Rosaline to pay attention to his subdued father.

'Um... lovely weather,' remarked Lady Honoria's husband as they sat down.

'Do not be silly, John, it is raining dreadfully,' she contradicted, while he relapsed into silence, vacantly sipping his wine. 'Madeleine, my dear, kindly excuse my husband's superfluous remarks.'

'Are most of your father's remarks superfluous?' asked Rupert in a whisper.

'Oh yes,' replied Rosaline. 'Mama considers that his primary use is in paying bills. What about your father?'

'We are very democratic: my mother listens to his views and then gives him a list of reasons why he is mistaken, but I wouldn't say he's under the thumb, luckily.'

'It is not necessarily an advantage. When a husband is under the thumb, as you put it, he does not need to bear the heavy burden of his own thoughts; indeed, it becomes unnecessary for him to have thoughts at all. Mama believes that this is chiefly responsible for Papa's excellent health,' she remarked seriously.

'What a dreadful philosophy!' cried Rupert. 'I'm rather attached to my thoughts, and I should be extremely sorry to part with them. If I ever get married, I shall stipulate beforehand my right to retain every one of my opinions.'

'How radical of you,' she laughed, 'but you say "if" as if the contingency were remote of your getting married.'

'Well, I suppose I shall at some point, but it's a bit early to think about it now. At any rate, the husband being under the thumb is hardly a prerequisite for a happy married life. Quite the opposite, in fact. Look at the Bishop of Barchester.'

'Yes, but you do not consider the opposite evil. Look at Tereus and Procne, Jason and Medea, Theseus and Ariadne.'

'In your first two examples, it was the husband who suffered more.'

'Precisely, which proves that it is for the benefit of husbands to obey their wives.'

'Very well, I concede,' Rupert laughed.

'Yes, indeed you must. An acquaintance begun with a concession promises to become a true political alliance.'

'Or a step towards marriage.'

'Of course,' she replied significantly.

'What do you mean, "of course"? I was making a joke.'

'Really Rupert, you are not very gallant.'

'That's because I'm too stunned to think of the correct things to say. I'm actually very good at being gallant to girls who are not very intelligent, but then I don't take the trouble to try,' he remarked.

'Well, at least that's honest, which is more than can be said for most boys. However, you are extraordinarily naive. Have you not realised why Mama has suddenly decided to visit you?'

'She and my mother are old friends.'

'Yes, but you've never met her before. I can see that I shall have to be very candid with you, which may not be quite ladylike,' Rosaline lowered her eyes modestly, then continued in a whisper, 'Mama is currently considering whether to put you on her list of eligible future husbands. I think you ought to be aware that this is extremely open-minded of her.'

'Good heavens! I'm glad you decided to be candid about it or I should be terribly perplexed. But don't you think I'm eligible?' he asked. 'I'm cleverer than I might appear, I assure you, it's just that you have a mesmerising effect on a chap which makes him suddenly become very silly.'

'I have no doubts about your personal eligibility for somebody, at any rate. My remark about Mama's open-mindedness was due to the fact that you have been educated by humans. Mama is very old school, you see, and, while she does not object to humans, she feels that our own culture should be preserved from the contaminating influence of theirs.'

'And what do you think about it?' asked Rupert.

'I haven't got any political opinions yet; I'm much more interested in music and literature than politics, but I am rather intrigued about humans. The only human I ever had close contact with was the dentist, so I don't really know much about them at all,' she observed. 'Rupert, tell me about the humans you know. What are they like?'

'Well, I had received an injunction from Mother not to tell school anecdotes, but I shall have to disobey it to please you,' he smiled. 'They're not that different from us really, except they have unusual taste in the arts these days and they are very fond of computers. Then again, there are vampires with bad taste too.'

'Indeed, I have noticed that at school, especially among the boys,' she replied.

'Also, if you want to fit in with them, it's very important to learn to use a mobile phone. Humans do not write letters, unless for an official purpose, and they communicate by mobile phone rather than telepathically. They have an extraordinary range of transiently fashionable vernacular, which you don't have to use but you do have to vaguely understand. Among teenage girls, it is best to talk about make-up, fashion and boys; among teenage boys, the standard topics are football, rugby and girls,' explained Rupert.

'Indeed? I do not think I should like to discuss such topics, and I can't imagine you fit in very well either.'

'Well, I tried for a bit, but I was so very incompetent at being a stereotypical teenage boy that everyone got annoyed. Then I decided just to be eccentric and true to myself, and after that I didn't make any more social errors,' he observed. 'Anyhow, that pleased my father very much, for he has always been very antisocial.'

'It sounds very interesting; I should like to see St Jude's very much' she said thoughtfully.

'I'm not sure you'd like it. It's very different from what you're accustomed to,' he interrupted hastily.

'Whether I would like it or not is not material: I should like to see it merely because I am curious. You know, Rupert,' she added confidingly, 'the human world has an irresistible fascination for me, but you mustn't let on to Mama, because she would disapprove. Sometimes we speculate about the humans at school, but nobody really quite knows what they are like.'

'Well, they have a great many misconceptions about us as well: all that sleeping in coffins, and drinking their blood,' replied Rupert.

'How very barbaric! It's been been over a thousand years since we drank human blood.'

'Precisely, but they are very much attached to the idea, just as Mr Mond is attached to the idea that I've got psychological issues. Humans are frightfully morbid.'

'I see,' said Rosaline. 'Mama says that they are very prejudiced and closed-minded. Have you experienced that?'

'Well, none of the other children know I'm a vampire, and I intend to keep it that way. It was easy until this week,' his eyes clouded slightly, and he sighed, 'but now my school life has been overturned by the arrival of a ghost.'

'Surely that doesn't matter, for humans can't see ghosts,' Rosaline pointed out.

'Well, that's what I thought, but my friend Ada saw her, or rather, heard her singing and playing the piano; I was there too, and she knows I've heard as well. I was rather hoping the ghost would just go away, but she seems to be trying to talk to Ada. She hasn't said anything, but I could tell she had had an enchanted dream.'

'It sounds very strange. What's she like?'

'Beautiful, and so clever and witty. When she plays the piano it's like the music of heaven. She understands me like nobody else does,' he gazed dreamily into the distance.

'I meant the ghost, actually,' laughed Rosaline, 'but now I'm very interested to meet your friend. She must be very beautiful to win your heart.'

'I never said anything to the effect that I was in love with her!' he cried, blushing. 'And I'm not, you know. I deny it officially, word of honour.'

'Then I am convinced it's true,' she teased, and he looked at her in the candlelight, realising all of a sudden that she was beautiful too. 'Whenever a boy says something to me on his word of honour, I know it must be false; but tell me what the ghost is like.'

'About seventeen, pretty, for a ghost, and she has a voice like an angel. She hasn't been dead for that long, not more than a decade, for she hadn't faded very much at all; I could see her quite distinctly, though Ada couldn't.'

'Was she from the school?'

'I don't know. I presume so, for she seemed very familiar with the piano.'

'What was she wearing?'

'Just ordinary clothes: a blouse and a skirt down to the knees. Why, does it matter?'

'Ghosts usually appear in the clothes they wore when they died,' she explained. 'You have been humanised, as Mama would say, if you didn't know that. If she was wearing her school clothes, which she must have been if the skirt was that long, then that suggests she died in or at least near to the school.'

'Do you think it was suicide?'

'It's possible, but unlikely. If she wanted to end her own life, why would her spirit linger? A tragic accident is more probable: that would explain why she would have some sort of unfinished business.'

'What sort of unfinished business?'

'Well, how should I know? I'm not Sherlock Holmes. It could be anything, though. There's a ghost at my school who haunts the classroom where he used to teach, because he had such a bossy wife that she ordered him to remain as a ghost if he died before her, but he's too frightened of her to haunt the house,' she said. 'He was young too, only three hundred years old, and we never found out how he died. It was very sudden, and he never talks about it, which is unusual. Most ghosts are very fond of talking about their deaths.'

'You know an awful lot about these things,' Rupert was impressed.

'Well, I've met quite a few ghosts. Anyway, there are plenty of books about all those sorts of things in the school library. The strange thing about your ghost, though, is that she has revealed herself to Ada,' said Rosaline thoughtfully. 'Is she of pure blood?'

'Pure blood?' he repeated.

'You know, is she all human, or is there some ancestor who was a witch or a vampire or something?'

'I don't think so, she seems completely normal and her parents are typical humans,' he replied.

'She may resemble a very distant ancestor. Sometimes these things are hidden for several generations,' she said. 'I just wondered, for it is very unusual indeed for a pure-blooded human to see ghosts, unless they have some connection with the deceased.'

'Well, I wouldn't know about that,' said Rupert, 'but it's all very exciting, isn't it? It's like being in a novel. The problem is, I don't know how to unravel the mystery without giving myself away. Ada is very observant, you see.'

'Rupert, I don't think the first conclusion she'll come to is that you're a vampire. She'd probably at most think you have psychological issues if you start behaving strangely,' she reassured him. 'But I do hope you will inform me about the progress of your investigation.'

'Of course,' smiled Rupert. 'If you have no objection, we could start a correspondence. It would be better if you wrote to me at school, since I'm there all week. Oh dear, I've forgotten the address… St Jude's Cathedral School…'

'Don't worry, my letters will get to you without the assistance of Royal Mail. If you fold yours into a bird shape and release them towards the setting sun, they will find me wherever I am.'

'Right-ho, I'll practise folding paper birds. My mother uses this method of communication frequently, but when I tried to do it before, my bird disintegrated before reaching its destination,' he said. 'However, I shall persevere.'

They both smiled conspiratorially at each other and the time flew by on silver wings till it was time to part. Indeed, Lady Honoria found that her daughter had such a favourable impression of Rupert that she was obliged to draw her attention to all his defects and to the very grave danger of his growing up to be like his father. In her opinion, dear Madeleine was far too indulgent in her management of her husband, and her taste in men had never been quite right, not even in her school days.

'But Mama, Rupert isn't my type at all,' Rosaline reassured her. 'He's very innocent and he doesn't try to flirt with me, which makes such a refreshing change.'

Meanwhile, Rupert's father was somewhat disgruntled that Rupert was quite willing to have a repeat of what he considered a very tedious evening, 'Whatever you do, don't marry the girl. She seems very nice but her mother is a harpy.'

'Don't be silly, Father, I have no designs upon her. I didn't even flirt with her! We talked about death and marriage.'

CHAPTER 4 - SAUSAGES AND SPECTRES

As the rosy fingers of the morning caressed the dreaming earth and the sun's rays flashed and danced on the spire of St Jude's Cathedral, a lone figure could be seen scuttling out of the school, a black dot on the landscape. The school was silent except for the languorous cooing of a pigeon, and lay nestled in the green curve of the hill, as if it were immersed in sweet slumber.

Miss Gourlay scurried along the cobbled path that wound beside the cathedral before slowing down meditatively as she came to the castle ruins. Glancing back to see that she was in fact alone, she climbed the precarious winding stair up to what was left of the east tower. The brisk autumn breeze swept wildly through the ruins, whistling in all the nooks and crannies, and serenading the dried leaves in an ecstatic dance. She gazed out at the snug little village which huddled in the castle's shadow, and, running her fingers over the rugged battlements, she closed her eyes briefly, summoning up the distant echoes of memory.

Suddenly, she turned around, startled, and saw that Mr Beanacre had followed her up to the tower. He did not appear quite as eccentric as usual, and they smiled at each other, as if there were some secret understanding between them.

'Well, Isolda, how do you find St Jude's?' he asked.

'It is very nice indeed; it has the romantic atmosphere of a time long past,' she replied.

For a moment, they stood dreamily on the top of the tower, each immersed in their own thoughts. They made a strange pair: the awkward, unhappy middle-aged man and the beautiful young woman. Presently, they left the castle and returned to the school, where the children were just saying goodbye to their parents.

'Rupert,' said Bertie, seeing them stroll off together amicably, 'I wonder what Miss Gourlay finds enjoyable in Mr Beanacre's company. Look, she's with him again.'

'I really can't imagine, unless she is educating him on physics,' laughed Rupert.

'She's a biology teacher, though,' objected Bertie.

'Which makes her more of an expert on physics than Mr Beanacre,' said Rupert decidedly. 'What do you girls think of her?'

'Oh, I like her,' remarked Beatrice. 'She's very friendly and she seems to be a good teacher.'

'I agree,' said Ada, 'and she seems to have settled in better than cover teachers normally do. For one thing, Mr Mond hasn't even asked her if she has psychological issues yet, and she has managed not to offend Dr Botherby.'

'That is an achievement, but I think we must give

credit to Mrs Johnson for organising Dr Botherby,' said Rupert. 'He wanted to have mixed ability English classes, you know, but she put a stop to it. Miss Gourlay has settled in remarkably quickly though, almost as if she'd been here before.'

'Yes,' agreed Bertie, 'but I have to say, her seating plans are dreadful.'

'I didn't think it was that bad,' said Beatrice.

'Well, it isn't for you, since your lab partner is a complete nondescript and you're close enough to Ada and Rupert to speak to them,' said Bertie, 'but I have to sit in between Becky and Lilly: it's unbearable!'

'You could just let them copy you,' suggested Ada.

'I do, but they complain about my handwriting being terrible.'

'It is terrible,' put in Rupert.

'I know, but even when I explain the answers to them, they still don't understand. And then they tell me off,' complained Bertie. 'I'm surrounded by girls, you know, so then they all join in.'

'Most boys would enjoy being surrounded by girls,' laughed Rupert.

'You might survive my seat, but no other boy would,' replied Bertie.

'Why is that?'

'Well, you're so conceited you wouldn't care when they tell you that you are unintelligent.'

'Well, I am intelligent, but not conceited,' Rupert countered, without having to consider for a moment. 'Anyway, it might be meant as a compliment.'

'How can the words, "Ethelbert, you are the thickest boy I have ever met" be interpreted as a compliment?'

Beatrice said, 'I genuinely think it might be, though, because those girls don't like nerdy boys like you and Rupert. They probably want to flirt with you.'

Bertie recoiled in horror, 'They don't! Sometimes they slap me!'

'Oh, so they do flirt with you, then,' said Beatrice gravely. 'Apparently, in state schools it's a recognised method of attracting a boy.'

'Well, that sort of thing would go on in state schools, I suppose, but I can't imagine the boys approve of the practice,' observed Bertie.

'And people accuse me of being a snob!' cried Rupert.

'Rupert, I have been to a state primary school, so I know what they are like. People don't like it if you're the slightest bit eccentric, or if you talk too much, or appear effeminate - and it's worse the older you get.'

'But you are effeminate, and you do talk a great deal,' teased Rupert.

'I'm not effeminate: I'm getting to be a proper tenor, and Mr Dodd said we both have to retire from the boy choristers after Christmas, but if we can manage to falsetto the high notes till the carol service, that would be good,' Bertie drew himself up indignantly. 'I think that state education is a very good thing, but that doesn't mean I want to be part of it, and you wouldn't survive a day, old chap.'

'Hmm..., I think you might be right,' said Rupert, 'but at least I have a normal name, so they might not think I was "posh" till they met me.'

'Bertie is not a very unusual name,' said Ada.

'No, but Ethelbert Hyacinth Jones is,' said Bertie.

'I see what you mean,' she said. 'Hyacinth is especially unfortunate, particularly when juxtaposed with Jones. Why did your mother call you that?'

'It was Aunt Caroline's idea, like most of my mother's ideas,' explained Bertie. 'You see, Aunt Caroline never got over the fact that we had such a common surname, so when I was born, she was determined to make up for it. And when Aunt Caroline is determined to do something, it would take an apocalypse to stop her.'

At that moment, the bell rang, and they parted company.

'See you in biology,' called Bertie. 'I will try to bear in mind the intended compliment when the girls are hitting me.'

Ada and Beatrice hastened to their form room on the third floor, where Mrs Johnson was arranging things. Having just returned from the rather chaotic jungle of papers and coffee cups in the staffroom, she found it soothing to ensure her own room was meticulously tidy. She too had noticed the pleasure which Mr Beanacre took in the company of her protégée - Miss Gourlay was now quite established in this role - but being perhaps more open-minded than the boys, she did not consider it particularly strange. In fact, she thought it an improvement on Mr Beanacre's usually antisocial disposition. In view of this and her recent victory over Dr Botherby, she was feeling extremely satisfied that morning.

'Good morning, girls, I think we shall have another rehearsal of Mr Mond's play this evening,' she announced, as Ada and Beatrice entered. 'Perhaps you could spread the word.'

'Yes, of course,' said Ada. 'By the by, rumour has it that Mr Mond's artistic temperament has been offended by the amendments we have made to the play. Mr Jury told me.'

'My dear,' said Mrs Johnson in a tone of authority, 'I shall, if necessary, politely remind Mr Mond that it is customary for each house to interpret individually the material provided by him, and that we are well within the limits of the custom. Besides, his latest work is an agglomeration of striking elements, none of them related, and some of them are positively indecent and highly inappropriate for young children. Do you, by any chance, know anything concerning the other houses and their rehearsals?'

'Well, I don't know what St Paul's are doing, but I have quite a lot of information about St Anthony's. According to Ernest, about half the cast have already lost their scripts, and he says it's about time their patron saint rallied round and miraculously produced them again, because the librarian has been disapproving of the amount of photocopying he's had to do.'

'Mr Jury also said,' added Beatrice, 'that Ernest expects him to do crowd control, just because he's Head of House, and he expects Ernest to do it, because he is supposed to be in charge of the play. The result is, that nobody does crowd control, Ernest is the laughing stock of the year sevens, and Mr Jury is perplexed as to what to do.'

'Poor Ernest,' said Mrs Johnson. 'I shall have a word with Mr Jury about him doing crowd control. That would explain why he recoiled in horror when I asked him if he was planning on applying to be a prefect at Easter.'

'I think,' smiled Ada, 'that Ernest would make a very good prefect, so long as his activities were restricted to only those not involving fuss of any description.'

Mrs Johnson admonished, 'Fuss is a necessary part of life: one is either fussing or being fussed at all times.'

Indeed, I think she must be correct about this fundamental component of life, for the staffroom was certainly full of it at all times. She did, as promised, remind a subdued Mr Jury that crowd control was a part of his duties as Head of House; he was not, however, completely subdued, as he did maintain his right to delegate fussing to Ernest.

'Only, he's not very good at it,' complained Mr Jury. 'The problem with Ernest is that he always tries to do everything to a high standard, including this play, when it would be so much easier and less stressful for everyone if he simply accepted that his cast is incompetent and the play is awful.'

'Mr Jury! I do hope you haven't expressed this opinion to Ernest. It may very well have occurred to him of its own accord, but it is of the utmost importance that we do not undermine the reputation of Mr Mond,' she informed the assembled staff gravely.

'Well, what's left of it,' said Mr Jury.

'What is quite remarkable is,' observed Mr Dodd, 'that Mr Mond's reputation is so very, what's the word I'm looking for? Resilient. I mean, you think it's in tatters, like the time he did a handstand in the middle of a lesson and broke the computer on his descent, but by the next week, his reputation has somehow miraculously repaired itself. If I did such a thing, I'm sure the Head would have reprimanded me severely.'

At that moment, the conversation was quickly stifled by the arrival of Mr Mond himself, with Dr Botherby following majestically behind. Having sat down and inspected the contents of the biscuit tin, the two deputy heads each gave an indication that they desired an audience: Mr Mond opened his mouth, and Dr Botherby pulled his scarf over his mouth. Then they both looked at each other reproachfully for a second, while the other teachers waited expectantly for their words of wisdom.

'Well?' demanded Mr Beanacre gruffly. 'What is it?'

'I have,' began Mr Mond, then corrected himself, 'Dr Botherby has made an important decision, which is, well, um...' he trailed off.

'What my learned friend wishes to say, intimate or communicate is, that I have, after much consultation, consideration and procrastination with Mr Mond, come to an important decision. I think I am expressing our collective opinion, that it is traditional, customary and necessary to censor, prohibit or, in short, ban, something at the beginning of every academic year,' here Dr Botherby paused impressively. 'The particular thing to be banned requires the careful consideration of a subtle, refined, and polished mind. I hope you will acquiesce to my opinion that, despite his good intentions, Mr Lloyd the caretaker's decision to ban ghosts in the music department was premature and controversial. Banning things, which is a fundamental part of the delicate art of school management, is not to be undertaken by anyone lightly, ill-advisedly or wantonly. I hereby come to the end of my short prologue and give you the substance of my discourse, which is that I have decided to ban...'

'Vegetarian sausages!' finished Mr Mond, unable to contain himself any longer.

The teachers were so astonished that there was a moment of complete silence - an event which had not occurred since 1939, when a no less important announcement was made.

Dr Botherby remarked snootily, pulling down his hat to show the extent of his displeasure, 'My learned friend has been somewhat too precipitate in his announcement, but we are indeed intending to ban vegetarian sausages.'

'But,' objected Mrs Johnson, 'what about those pupils who are vegetarian?'

'They will instead consume vegetarian meat - substitute cylinders,' explained Dr Botherby solemnly.

'What is the difference between those and vegetarian sausages, Dr Botherby?' asked Miss Gourlay innocently.

Flattered, Dr Botherby replied, 'Only the name! Is it

not, if I may say so myself, rather ingenious? We have, you see, in this way, succeeded in banning something without actually banning it. It is unprecedented in the history of St Jude's.'

'It was my idea too,' added Mr Mond. 'I was inspired by the EU. You know, the Head feels that we should do our bit to make young people more politically aware, and of course we must ban something, so this scheme kills two birds with one stone. I shall bring it up to the Head at the next staff meeting; I am hoping she'll approve.'

The teachers considered all this very gravely, though Mr Jury did utter a peal of unholy laughter, which he promptly disguised as a cough. However, he was at once reprimanded for his unbecoming frivolity by Dr Botherby, who showed his disapprobation by polishing and replacing his glasses with much solemnity. As you may have gathered by now, dear reader, Dr Botherby always covered up some part of his illustrious person, when he wanted to appear imposing, as if to shelter it from the contamination of irreverent listeners or barking dogs, like one of Gratiano's dumb wise men. However, there being no part of him still uncovered at this point, he was obliged to resort to his glasses, over the top of which he now peered like a haughty but slightly disconcerted owl.

Meanwhile, Mr Mond contemplated with satisfaction the success of the scheme, and was only the tiniest bit resentful that Dr Botherby had not let him speak. Nevertheless, he thought innocently, great scholars must be allowed their little idiosyncrasies.

Though occasionally disgruntled by Dr Botherby's attempts to take over the pastoral affairs of St Jude's, he was unswerving in his faith in the latter's mental brilliance.

That evening, rehearsals for Mr Mond's play resumed, but the renowned playwright decided all of a sudden to leave the child of his imagination to others to interpret after all. We can only presume that Mrs Johnson's words of wisdom had their effect. Mr Jury was somewhat exasperated to find that the assembly hall had been invaded by an army of percussion instruments, but she magnanimously allowed him to rehearse on the other side of the theatre.

'Now,' said Mrs Johnson, 'I would like us to begin from the start of Act Two. Archie, are you listening?'

'Yes, Mrs Johnson, I am,' cried a small boy in great alarm.

'I was in fact addressing a different Archie, but I am glad to hear it. Right, let us begin. Mr Jury!' she called.

'Oh, yes,' said Mr Jury hastily. 'Everybody be quiet! Right, Ernest, I'll leave the actual directing to you.'

'Thanks, Mr Jury,' said Ernest gratefully, mildly astonished that the Latin teacher had decided to do some crowd control after all.

'Oh, my darling,' sighed Ada, fainting a little awkwardly into Archie's arms, because he was not paying attention, and there was a very real danger he might drop her.

'Archie!' cried Mrs Johnson reproachfully. 'Ada, could you please faint again? Thank you.'

On the other side of the theatre, Rupert whispered

to Bertie, 'I always thought that he was very phlegmatic. I mean, since this is probably the only time he'll ever get to put his arms round a pretty girl, you'd think he would make the most of it: I would!'

Ada fainted again as requested, 'Oh, my darling, my life has become but a barren sea of sorrow since my father has so cruelly separated us. Even now he may discover us, and then there will be no limit to his wrath. I am sure I will die!'

'But Leonora, you are in excellent health. I really don't think you need to be so dramatic' said Archie.

'Heartless, unfeeling man! When you are not by my side, I fade and languish like a withered flower, and yet you seem to manage quite well without my company. You can never understand my feelings; men are so very insensible, more so than the cockled horns of the tender snail,' she had said all this very passionately, but then she broke off. 'Mrs Johnson, that can't possibly be right. I mean to say, we can just about tolerate the barren sea of sorrow, but that last line is just too badly garbled.'

'Yes, you're quite right,' affirmed Mrs Johnson. 'What do you think he meant to say?'

'Well, it sounds like he's trying to quote Love's Labours Lost: "love is more soft and sensible than the tender horns of the cockled snail." However, that doesn't at all fit with my complaint about him being unfeeling. I think,' said Ada thoughtfully, 'that it might just work if I said "men are so very insensible; they are strangers to love, which is as soft and sensible as the tender horns of the cockled snail." What do you think, Mrs Johnson?'

'That sounds excellent, and it is very true.'

'Mrs Johnson!' cried Archie urgently.

'What is the matter now, Archie?'

'It says in the stage directions that I have to kiss her! I don't have to, do I? My mother would tell me off if I did, you know.'

'Do not be silly, Archie,' Mrs Johnson said majestically. 'You are positively forbidden to kiss her.'

At this point, the phlegmatic Archie breathed a sigh of relief and looked around vacantly.

'I implore you to take me away with you,' continued Ada. 'Alas, I am so frail, but love will give me wings to flee these bleak walls and fly away with you to some better land. Archie!' she added in a whisper.

'Oh!' cried the latter. 'My dear, I shall elope with you tonight, but I ought to go now to check the train timetable and buy the tickets. I'm awfully hard up, so we'll have to travel second class. But tell me, Leonora, do you truly love me with all your heart? Women are fickle, you know, and I have heard that the errant knight Sir Jeremy has been paying you much attention.'

Having struggled through this difficult passage, Archie waited expectantly for Ada to faint again, as it said in the script. However, she seemed to be spiritually somewhere far away, for she was gazing at the other end of the stage as if she were hypnotised, and she was not paying the slightest attention to poor Archie.

She was not looking at anything in particular, as

there was nothing there. Yet something in the room seemed to have changed: the air pressed around her with cold fingers, and all of a sudden it seemed to be dusk, but clearly nobody else could sense this. For a moment, she could almost discern a presence; there was no physical shape to it, just an area that seemed darker and colder, like the air in a graveyard. Rupert was standing right next to it, and she caught his eye for a split second. Then it was gone.

A little confused, she fainted again into Archie's arms, but this time mechanically, for her heart was no longer in the play.

Meanwhile, Rupert wandered behind the curtain - he was not required in the scene being rehearsed at that moment - and the ghost followed him.

'What are you trying to do?' asked Rupert reproachfully. 'You know, all sorts of problems occur when ghosts start revealing themselves to humans, and it's really quite unnecessary.'

'Well,' she replied in a slightly offended tone, 'there was no need for you to interfere and stop her from sensing my presence. Had you waited a few minutes, I should have absorbed enough energy from the surroundings to communicate with her, if only briefly.'

'Yes, but why do you want to communicate with her?'

'Because I want to find out about my death, and I feel instinctively that she can help me. It's sort of as if we're kindred spirits.'

'Yes, I can see that,' admitted Rupert, 'but I don't see how she can help you. That time we heard you singing, she was very disturbed, because, of course, she knows nothing about supernatural beings.'

'Well, you ought to enlighten her then, Rupert,' she said. 'At any rate, if she's going to find out that you're a vampire, then she had better find out from your own lips.'

'But she wouldn't find out of her own accord. Really,' Rupert tried to look solemn, 'I would be very much upset if you told her.'

'Goodbye, Rupert,' she said. 'You will keep your word, won't you?'

'Well, I didn't think I had promised anything, but...' began Rupert. 'Come back! I have so much to ask you.'

However, she had faded away into the air, leaving only a faint impression behind her, almost like an echo. Sighing, he slipped out from behind the curtain and tried, not very successfully, to be enthusiastic about Mr Mond's play. The whole affair was very awkward, he thought. Throughout the rehearsal, his bright eyes kept darting over to Ada, with a kind of furtive pleasure. The thought that their intimacy might be shattered if the ghost led her to discover his true identity pressed like a lead weight upon him.

That night, Ada dreamed again about the ghost. Almost as soon as she fell asleep and the school drifted into focus, she knew that Margaret was near. This time, she waited patiently and did not allow herself to come into contact with anybody, in case it caused the dream to suddenly end. She felt very light and insubstantial, as if she were walking on air.

Drifting along a little aimlessly, she found herself in the school chapel. Sunlight streamed through the stained glass windows, dappling the stone floor with splashes of colour. The dying rays of the sun illuminated the sculpted angel hovering above, drenching his wings in gold. The familiar droning of the organ accompanying the choir washed over Ada. She glanced round the choir: a few of the younger choristers seemed vaguely familiar but she could not be sure. Then she caught sight of Margaret, and their eyes met, with a look as if there were some secret understanding between them. Everybody else was oblivious to her presence, but it seemed as though Margaret was guiding her through her dreams, trying to tell her something.

As evensong came to an end, she exchanged a few commonplace remarks with the others, then wandered out of the chapel with her friend, whose face Ada could not quite see. They were conversing in low voices, and as they walked, their voices grew fainter. They began slowly to blur with the surroundings, till everything rippled and wavered, as if she were looking at the bottom of a brook. She tried to clutch at the dream, but it kept on fading.

Suddenly, it shot back into focus for a moment, but the scene had changed. Margaret and her friend were at the foot of the castle ruins. The other girl was crying quietly, and Margaret was trying in vain to console her.

Then the dream vanished all of a sudden, and Ada woke up, her heart racing. Darkness enveloped the dormitory, smothering it in an ominous silence. At that moment, she was quite certain that this was no ordinary dream, but a message from the ghost, and as she was wondering how this could be, she sank into a deep, oblivious sleep.

CHAPTER 5 - A SERIES OF REVELATIONS

As soon as he saw Ada at breakfast the next morning, Rupert knew that she had had another dream. Buttering his toast absent-mindedly, so that quite as much butter attached itself to the plate as to the toast, he debated anxiously with himself what to do.

'How did you sleep last night?' he asked at last, trying to sound casual.

'Not that well, actually: I had the most peculiar dream, in which I saw Margaret,' she began.

'Margaret, is that her name?' he interrupted hastily. 'The ghost whom we heard in room eight, I mean.'

'Yes,' she replied. 'Rupert, do you really think there is a ghost? It's not just a figment of my imagination?'

'Not at all. The ghost definitely exists,' said Rupert firmly. 'After all, we couldn't have both imagined exactly the same thing.'

'Good heavens!' cried Bertie. 'I didn't think you two would believe in ghosts. I must admit, what happened in the music department was rather strange, but there must be some rational explanation.'

'Bertie,' said Rupert, 'it's not a question of believing but of opening your eyes to what is right in front of you, no matter how extraordinary it may seem. Look, we need to get to House Assembly now; after English, it's break time, so we'll talk then.'

'Alright, we'll see you then on the usual bench,' said Ada.

'No, it's too public,' objected Rupert. 'After English, you two girls, don't bother to wait for us - we'll be a bit slow packing up - but we'll rejoin you behind the organ in the chapel. Nobody ever goes in there at that time, but it's not technically forbidden.'

With that, he got up and hurried off, followed by Bertie, leaving the girls thoroughly mystified. However, his strange behaviour confirmed Ada in the opinion that he had some dark secret. As she watched his dark head receding into the crowd, she wondered what it might be with a shiver of anticipation.

As soon as the bell rang for break, Ada and Beatrice merged themselves into the crowd, before drifting away furtively into the chapel. A few minutes later, they heard a clatter of footsteps and the boys joined them. All four sat down on the edge of the altar steps, where they were screened from view by the organ. For a moment, they preserved an expectant silence, broken only by Bertie nibbling a biscuit with an expression of profound wisdom.

'Well, Rupert, don't be so mysterious,' he said at last.

Rupert began nervously, clasping and unclasping

his hands, 'Well, what I'm about to say is probably going to sound fantastical, but I assure you solemnly that I've never been more serious in all my life,' he took a deep breath and continued, 'Do you remember when Mr Lloyd banned ghosts in the music department, and we all thought it was rather amusing? Well, it turns out he was quite right: there is a ghost. Her name is Margaret, apparently, for I think, Ada, that your dreams are quite correct. She was a pupil here, and she died, how exactly nobody knows, not even herself. But since then, something has occurred very recently to reawaken her dormant spirit, and she is trying to make contact with us in order to solve the mystery of her own death.'

'Are you serious?' Bertie's eyes expanded even further.

'Yes. You must all think I've gone completely mad,' said Rupert, a little crossly. 'I thought this might happen.'

'No, I don't think you're mad,' replied Ada, 'for I'm quite sure I saw her yesterday at rehearsals; well, I couldn't see anything, I just sensed a presence.'

'Was that when you suddenly became sort of captivated and went into a kind of trance, when you were supposed to faint into Archie's arms?' asked Beatrice.

'Yes, didn't you notice it?'

'No, I couldn't sense anything unusual, but you did look like you'd literally seen a ghost.'

'Rupert,' said Ada, 'you saw her too, didn't you?'

'Yes,' said Rupert gravely.

'And then he went behind the curtain and seemed

to be muttering to himself,' cried Bertie excitedly. 'Were you talking to this ghost then? But how?'

'Yes, I spoke to her,' said Rupert in a low voice, studying the floor intently. 'The answer to the second question is a rather awkward one. I don't want you to be alarmed. I want you all to still be my friends, as we were before.'

'It's alright, old chap, out with it. It can't be that bad,' said Bertie cheerfully.

'I'm…' he stuttered, then looked up and announced falteringly, 'I'm a vampire.'

They all stared at him, stunned. Looking anxiously at them all, he bared his fangs.

'You see, it's true,' he said quietly. 'I'm a vampire.'

'Good heavens!' murmured Bertie. 'I never thought ghosts or vampires existed.'

'Well, they do, and so do witches and werewolves and many other groups of supernatural beings.'

'I say, it's extraordinary,' said Bertie. 'But Rupert, how have I not noticed the fangs before?'

'Because they are retractable, rather like a cat's claws,' explained Rupert, 'and it's not considered good etiquette to show your fangs when among humans. By the way, an important point I would like to clear up: I neither sleep in a coffin, nor drink human blood, and I am very fond of sunshine.'

'So, you're not like Dracula, then?' asked Bertie, anxiously scrutinising him.

'Certainly not!' cried Rupert indignantly. 'Dracula is a very slanderous book which I thoroughly disapprove of. There are, of course, evil vampires who may do all those things they do in books, but they are a minority. You see, now I've told you, you'll never regard me in the same way. It's not that I'm ashamed of what I am,' he added defiantly, 'but, oh I wish I hadn't told you.'

'Don't be silly, Rupert,' said Ada consolingly, 'You're still the same whether you're a vampire or not: still our friend.'

'Yes, our friend always,' the other two agreed.

'Thanks,' he breathed a sigh of relief, and, retracting his fangs, smiled at his friends radiantly. 'Well, sit closer to me again: you've all been gradually edging away during the last part of the conversation, as if you were afraid.'

'Wouldn't you be, if you suddenly found out that your best friend was a vampire and might drink your blood?' said Bertie.

'I suppose so,' Rupert conceded. 'At any rate, the drinking of human blood has been illegal for some considerable time, that is, ever since the vampire government decided to integrate with the humans.'

'Don't you drink blood at all, then?'

'Well, yes, but not from humans. There's no need to look like that: I don't see that drinking the blood of animals is really worse than eating them!' cried Rupert, and as the others considered this, he added, 'But these days you can get tablets which act as a blood substitute, so I take those in school. My father's a chemist, among other things, and he makes the tablets, as well as potions for all sorts of purposes.'

'I always thought vampires were uncivilised, you

know,' remarked Bertie, 'but apparently I was mistaken.'

'Well, in some ways we're more civilised than humans: for one thing, we don't have all these interminable wars,' observed Rupert. 'And before you ask the next question, yes, I am perfectly fine being in a chapel - the church of England is very open-minded, and all my years of being a boy chorister have led to no ill effects on my health.'

'How did you know I was going to ask that?' asked Bertie, impressed.

'I always know what you're thinking, old chap,' said Rupert. 'Mind reading takes some practice, like everything else, but I've always found it much easier with the male of the species.'

'Probably because your minds are much more simple,' suggested Ada.

'Probably,' agreed Rupert. 'Anyway, let's get back to the point. What do we know about Margaret?'

'Not much, really,' said Ada. 'She was a chorister, though, so I suppose we can find out something from Mr Dodd.'

'Wouldn't it look a bit odd, asking him about a ghost?' asked Beatrice.

'We'll get around that when we come to it,' Rupert waved this issue away dismissively. 'Anyhow, I can do the interrogation if you prefer; since I have a reputation for being odd, it shouldn't much matter.'

'I've just thought of something,' said Ada suddenly. 'There's probably a memorial plaque either here or in the Cathedral, but most likely here.'

'I've been here countless times, and I've never seen it,' objected Bertie.

'Well, you probably weren't looking,' pointed out Rupert. 'It would be something small, discreet, but it can't be that hard to find.'

He got up and surveyed the chapel carefully, then announced after a little while, 'I've found it. I never noticed it before, because I've always got my back to it in evensong,' he indicated a small brass plaque above the choir stalls and read, 'In loving memory of Margaret Harding, 1997-2014. Rest in peace. So, she died five years ago; she was in either year twelve or thirteen. It doesn't tell us much, really, but at least it's recent enough for people to remember.'

'Who can we ask about her, though?' asked Bertie.

'Ernest,' said Ada suddenly. 'Ernest would have been in his first year when she died. And it would be very easy to ask him about it, for he's not of a very inquisitive turn of mind and would think nothing of it.'

'Would he remember, though? I mean, I don't think I'd be able to give you a detailed account of the life of anyone who was in the sixth form when I was in year seven,' remarked Bertie dubiously.

'Don't be silly, Bertie,' interjected Rupert. 'If any of them had died, I'm sure you'd remember that.'

'Oh, I see what you mean,' he replied. 'We can ask him in orchestra at lunch time.'

At that moment, they were startled by the shriek of the school bell and hurried off to lessons. Rupert glanced back at the quaint little chapel, quietly contemplating the secrets held within its walls. He had deposited his own secret - which could hardly be called a secret anymore - in its sanctuary, and this made his heart as light as air, almost as if he really belonged here.

Following a hurried lunch, the four friends went to orchestra. When they passed the piano rooms, they all shivered involuntarily, as they wondered if the ghost would appear. However, the only sound was of somebody attempting to tune a trumpet, so they pressed on to Mr Finchby's room, which was unusually quiet, apart from the trumpet, due to the absence of the eminent Director of Music.

'Try a little sharper,' suggested Ernest to the trumpet player. 'No, Nigel, that sounds even worse. For heaven's sake, just tune it with the piano: I know we're not supposed to touch it, on pain of banishment, but I'll vouch for it that your fingers are clean if he comes in.'

'Ernest,' replied Nigel anxiously, 'I am really rather afraid that Mr Finchby will spontaneously combust. You see, I'm always managing to upset him somehow, though I don't mean to: he's already displeased with me because I refused to play the euphonium for the junior orchestra.'

'Well, if you wanted to stay in his good books, you could have obliged him,' remarked Rupert, coming in. 'I know a euphonium is not considered a very respectable instrument, but it can't be much worse than a trumpet.'

Nigel replied haughtily, 'There is a world of difference between them. That's like saying there's no difference between a violin and a viola, but we brass players have our integrity too.'

'Indeed? That's news to me,' laughed Ernest, throwing him a chocolate bar. 'They are new,' he added, 'and as edible as they'll ever be. Does the integrity of brass players by any chance consist of making it a point of honour to play fortissimo and slightly out of tune at all times?'

'We're not always out of tune,' protested Nigel. 'By the way, we have a new french horn, so wish me luck: he moved to our sixth form from the local comprehensive, and he's in my form. Now, I don't want to sound snobbish, but that's hardly a good omen.'

'Nigel, you are tuning the wrong way. You are almost a quarter tone too sharp,' observed Ada.

'Ernest!' said Nigel reproachfully. 'Ada, will you give me the note, please? Thanks, I've sorted it out now. I must say, you're much easier to tune to than those tuning apps for phones.'

'Really, Nigel, what a compliment to give to a girl! You'll have to do better than that to attract the new girls,' Ernest smiled slyly. 'Now you've sorted the trumpet out, will you please give out the brass folders; I've done strings; Bertie can do woodwind, since it's his section.'

Nigel did so, then exclaimed, having looked inside his folder, 'Good heavens! Have you seen what the music is? You're not going to believe this.'

'Prokofiev?' suggested Rupert, raising an eyebrow.

'Fortunately not,' replied Nigel. 'It is a piece written by the director of music himself, but the strange thing about it, is that it starts off sounding a bit like Wagner, and then there's a bit with far too many dissonances for my liking, and at the end we seem to have completely lost the plot.'

'It looks atonal at the end,' observed Ada.

'Precisely: he's lost the plot.'

'Nigel, you must not offend people by making judgemental remarks,' Rupert admonished in his best imitation of Mrs Johnson. 'It's certainly highly original and striking.'

At that moment, Mr Finchby himself bustled in, glowering like a storm cloud. However, having only heard the tail end of Rupert's remark, he interpreted it as a compliment, and the sun transiently broke through the dark clouds. This was only fleeting, though, for he then proceeded to express his disapproval of everything in the department with much acerbity.

'Rupert,' said Ernest, 'may I borrow your rosin?'

'Here you are,' he replied, getting it out of his violin case. 'Ernest, I have an important question to ask you.'

'Ask away, old chap,' Ernest put rosin on his bow.

'Do you remember a girl called Margaret Harding?'

'How could I forget her? She died very tragically when I was in year seven,' whispered Ernest.

'What was the extent of your acquaintance with her?'

'Rupert, you sound like an inquisitor,' admonished Ada quietly. 'That's not at all how to go about it.'

'Oh, I didn't know her well at all, but naturally I was rather shocked when she died,' said Ernest. 'Why do you want to know, anyway?'

Rupert hesitated and Ada interjected quickly, 'I've often wondered about the plaque in the chapel; just idle curiosity really, but I feel a sort of interest in her. She died so young.'

'Ah,' sighed Ernest, 'most people don't notice the plaque, and anyone who knew her intimately has long since left the school. Poor Margaret, she has faded away, almost into oblivion. None of us ever dreamed she would...' he lowered his voice, 'that she would commit suicide.'

'How do you know she did?' inquired Rupert. 'What happened?'

'The whole affair was hushed up, so I really don't know, but apparently, it could not be doubted that it was suicide. And only a few days before, she had been so happy; but it only goes to show how well concealed psychological issues may be.'

'Indeed, it is very tragic,' said Ada. 'But you thought she was happy?'

'Well, she was always happy in rehearsals for House Singing, which was the only time I really ever spoke to her. She had a voice like an angel. It was brilliant, the way she trained the choir, and she always had a smile and a kind word, even for the most out of tune of the Lilliputians, of which I may have been one,' he smiled in a melancholy way. 'We won House singing that year, and then, a few days after her great triumph, she died.'

'Was she lonely, do you think?' asked Rupert.

'Definitely not,' said Ernest. 'She was very quiet,

not exactly one of the popular girls - she wasn't frivolous enough - but nobody could think anything ill of her. Being pretty as well as agreeable, she had quite a few admirers in the choir, though I don't think she favoured any of them above the others. I wouldn't know about that, she was too much older than me.'

'And yet,' observed Rupert, 'a girl may have many male admirers and no female enemies but still be lonely, without some intimate relationship.'

'Oh, but she had that,' said Ernest. 'There was a girl in her class, Isolda, and she and Margaret were inseparable. She was heartbroken when it happened, so much so that I think Mr Mond got quite worried, and with reason - before her friend died, she was eccentric, and afterwards, well, her grief turned mere strangeness almost to a kind of insanity. I think she recovered, though; she went to Oxford.'

The conversation was abruptly cut short by Mr Finchby beginning the rehearsal; his conducting technique was really most remarkable, so I feel the urge to mention it. It chiefly consisted of attacking the front desks with his baton, jumping up and down and making peculiar faces. As the orchestra struggled through his magnum opus and screeched painfully to the climax, he turned as red as a lobster and stood on one leg, leaning forwards impressively. Having reprimanded them for not being in time, he then proceeded to tap the beats on his stand with a twitching movement verging on the neurotic.

At last, the rehearsal finished, and the children dispersed for afternoon lessons. As they queued up for physics, Rupert shuddered and announced, 'That was the most painful musical experience of my life. The very pegs of my violin were so traumatised that they slipped, a thing which never happens.'

'I think all our instruments will be traumatised by the time we perform this piece,' replied Beatrice. 'I don't like to think what my mother would say if she found out I have to strike my cello with the wood of my bow in bars forty-five to sixty.'

'It is, as Rupert said, very striking,' said Ada emphatically.

'Yes, there's no other way to put it diplomatically,' Bertie agreed, 'but I must say, Rupert, you're awfully lucky.'

'In what way?'

'Well, you never get overheard making judgemental remarks, so all the teachers mistakenly think you are very mild and placid,' he explained.

'That's not luck at all, you simply have to keep your ears open,' said Rupert. 'I heard the footsteps of Mr Finchby as he walked up the steps to the music building. Anyway, we have information about Margaret.'

After Ada had enlightened them, Berte remarked, 'It's very strange, though. I mean, you can't commit suicide without knowing about it, can you?'

'You could if you'd been hypnotised,' said Rupert, 'but a less fantastical explanation, is that the coroner was simply wrong.'

'Yes, probably that's it,' agreed Bertie. 'After all, I don't see how anyone would have had the chance to hypnotise her while she was boarding here.'

'It would be easy, though, for a witch or something to control her mind. You don't need much time for that,' said Rupert. 'If I wanted to murder someone, that's how I would do it: no human coroner would ever find out the truth.'

'But why would anyone want to murder Margaret?' asked Beatrice. 'There would be no benefit to it.'

'Well, we don't know that,' said Rupert. 'There are many things we don't know about her, and one of them may furnish a motive. She may not even know herself. I think we can definitely rule out suicide; an accident is still a possibility, but then again, one would think she'd know if it was.'

'For the coroner to think it was suicide and be so firmly convinced about it, there must have been some apparently conclusive evidence,' mused Ada, 'like a note or something. Rupert, couldn't you ask her about what she was doing when she died?'

'I don't think she is particularly keen on communicating with me,' he replied. 'At any rate, if this is, as I suspect, a supernatural murder, she probably wouldn't remember. At least, not consciously. However, you may discover something in one of your dreams. I feel that they are the best clues we have to go on.'

'If only her friend, Isolda, were still in the school, she might be able to enlighten us about her life, family circumstances and so on,' remarked Ada. 'But she would have finished Oxford and started working by now.'

'It's an unusual name, isn't it?' said Bertie.

'Yes, it is, rather,' said Rupert, 'but even so, I don't think we'd be able to find her. There must be a fairly large number of people called Isolda in the whole of Britain, and we wouldn't know where to start looking. She could have gone abroad, for all we know.'

'True,' said Bertie. 'Anyway, it would be rather strange to telephone her and ask her about her dead friend who is now a ghost and might have been murdered. She'd think we were mad.'

'Indeed,' chuckled Rupert, then looking serious again, 'but I feel instinctively that she holds the key to this mystery. Do you not think, that her grief which was verging on insanity is partly a result of some painful knowledge? Don't ask me how I am sure of this; but sure of it I am, as sure as I am that Margaret did not commit suicide.'

At that moment, Mr Beanacre opened the door and growled his permission for the class to enter. It seemed to Rupert that he started at the name of Margaret, but this could have been merely a coincidence, for he had a habit of twitching constantly. Ever since that first lesson, the enigmatic physics teacher seemed to have taken a dislike to him. This was not especially obvious in his demeanour, considering that he was rather unfriendly and severe to all his students. However, Rupert was sensitive to such things, though he seemed obtuse at times, and he could feel in the air a kind of tension, which seemed only to increase after this incident.

That evening, having brooded over the mystery all through prep, he decided to write to Rosaline and ask her opinion. Taking a sheet of parchment, which he had brought from home, he hesitated for a moment with his fountain pen poised above the paper. His fingers gripped it nervously for no reason. All of a sudden, he felt unsure of himself, and words, usually so abundant, fled from his pen.

'Hello, Rupert,' one of the other boys ambled into the room, and he turned pale in spite of himself. 'What are you writing so secretly?' he asked teasingly. 'A love letter?'

'Certainly not,' replied Rupert haughtily. 'And it's not secret.'

'Well, who are you writing to, then?'

'If you must know, the person to whom I am writing is my cousin,' he lied smoothly, 'and, no, I can't text her because her phone is broken, and I can't email her, because I only have a school email address.'

'Oh, I see. I'll leave you to it, in that case,' he wandered off aimlessly, shaking his head slightly at the eccentricity of a boy who, in the twenty-first century, would write letters to his cousin; he was also a little disappointed that it was not a love letter, for this would have been food for gossip.

However, this interruption reminded Rupert that he ought to write his letter quickly, and so he began, a little feverishly, for he was not quite sure about the correct way to write to ladies.

23rd September

Dear Rosaline,

I hope this letter finds you in good health and high spirits. As promised last weekend, when I had the pleasure of meeting you, I am including for your consideration the results of my investigations so far.

You know, you were quite right about Ada not suspecting my identity, but I ended up telling her, and she was OK with it, so all is well. She had another dream, and then the ghost, Margaret, turned up in one of our rehearsals of Mr Mond's play.

The play, by the way, is, quite frankly, dreadful and modern. During one scene, which we recently ran through, I was obliged to fly into an ecstasy of adoration for my beautiful mistress - I am playing the page, but, alas, she is not beautiful - and then the husband is supposed to enter, whilst I hide under the bed. This, to my mind, seems to be just a poor imitation of the Marriage of Figaro, but with a bed instead of an armchair. No doubt, it was meant to be romantic, but it wasn't, because she told me off in the middle of it, for a reason which I can't ascertain. That's girls for you!

Anyhow, I am wandering from the matter of my discourse. Having interrogated Ernest, we have discovered that her death was suicide and that there was no doubt about it. However, I am not at all inclined to believe this, and indeed, this case strikes me as sinister. I feel instinctively that something supernatural was at work, though I am completely at a loss as to the motive behind what I suspect is murder. Do tell me what steps you think we should pursue.

Oh, just one more thing on this case. Margaret had a very intimate friend called Isolda, who was, again according to Ernest, very eccentric. She was much grieved by her friend's supposed suicide, but Ernest said he thinks she rose out of the depths of sorrow when she went to Oxford. Ada thinks that this friend of Margaret's plays an important role in the story, and I think she's right, for apparently she appears in the dreams, but Ada can not see her face. This is unusual, don't you think? I don't know anything really about the interpretation of dreams; perhaps you could enlighten me?

Adieu, ma belle amie. Je pense à vous toujours. Venez me voir bientôt, ou apprenez-moi à vivre où vous n'êtes pas.

Votre tendre ami,

Rupert

P.S. Mr Beanacre, the physics teacher whom I told you about, was even more irate than usual today. He happened to overhear me discussing the case. I do not know if these two circumstances are related; probably not.

When he had written the post script, he read through the letter again and felt that it was somewhat awkward. However, time was short, and he reflected that in real life, people do not do things as they do in books, so there was no reason why they should write literary letters either. Then another problem occurred to him: the paper was not square, so he could not fold it into a bird as instructed, unless he cut off the end. This difficulty caused him some annoyance, as Rosaline must think him very silly indeed if she ever found out about it. The only thing to be done was to try to fold it anyway; he began this apprehensively, for he was not particularly skilled in the folding of paper birds at the best of times.

Suddenly, to his delight, the parchment adjusted itself into the required square, and he managed the rest without too much trouble. When he had finished, he drew an eye on the bird and waited hopefully.

'I need two eyes, silly boy,' the bird chirped in a rather disgruntled tone, wobbling on the desk.

'Sorry,' said Rupert, drawing the second eye on. 'Do keep still, please. Done. Now, fly to Rosaline as quickly as you can.'

Checking that nobody was watching, he opened the window and released the bird. It fluttered rather awkwardly for a moment, unsure of itself, and indeed it did look rather ungainly. Then the dying rays of the sun drenched its wings in mellow, golden light, and it soared off into the distance. Rupert wondered what Rosaline was doing and how everything was at the castle, wishing for a moment that he was like other vampires, as he recalled how she had laughed at his ignorance. He sighed as he watched the bird go until it faded into a speck, then blended with the evening itself.

CHAPTER 6 - THE COLOSSEUM AND THE CLUES

The next morning, as Rupert was getting dressed, he could not help glancing almost constantly at the window, wondering if there would come a letter from Rosaline. He replied only in vague monosyllables to the remarks of the boys with whom he shared the dormitory, and Bertie kept on looking at him inquiringly. Just as he found himself unable to procrastinate any longer, he discerned a faint tapping sound at the window, so quiet that no human would have been able to hear it. Languidly, as if there were no particular reason for him to do so, he opened the window and surveyed the school grounds. Then he remarked to the others that it looked like rain, and suggested that they go down to breakfast at once.

Bertie, mystified, whispered as they sauntered down the grand staircase of mahogany, 'Rupert, what is going on? I can tell by your smile that you are up to something.'

'I'll explain later,' said Rupert, happily feeling the parchment bird nestled in his pocket. 'Now please pretend to be normal.'

'I am normal,' retorted Bertie emphatically.

As soon as he got a moment to himself, Rupert unfolded the letter and read breathlessly.

Dear Rupert,

Your letter amused me very much indeed; it quite brightened up what had been a rather mundane day, and I must confess that it is quite a curiosity among the other uninteresting letters which I receive. It flew here safely, although it did collapse onto my desk with a rather forlorn air, complaining that you had not folded it properly.

I am very intrigued by what you have told me regarding the case, and I think you ought to trust your instinct, if you sense something sinister about it. What you wrote about Ada's dreams is rather strange. For one thing, it is most unusual for a human to receive such dreams in the first place, for these are not ordinary dreams, but a message from the ghost, Margaret. What you describe about her friend, Isolda, being always present but never seen, is also very strange. As far as I am aware, this could only be the result of somebody else intercepting and interfering with the dream before it reaches her, which of course begs the question of who would want to do this and for what reason. Once we have worked this out, we will be close to penetrating the heart of the mystery.

I am afraid I am quite ignorant too, on the subject

of dreams, for it is a branch of magic which not many vampires these days practise. In most places, the art of manipulating dreams has been lost or at least degenerated, except perhaps in a few old families who are endowed with the gift. As my mother frequently informs me, this is the price we have to pay for social integration.

However, I shall do some research on the subject in the school library when I have time, for the dreams seem to be, as you say, the key to the matter. By the by, I should very much like to meet your friend Ada, not only for the purpose of socialising, but also to discuss this point. I wonder if this could somehow be arranged, for I am doubtful whether telepathic communication would work, although she does not seem quite like ordinary humans.

Just before I end this epistle, I am sure you will not be offended if I give you a little advice on the art of writing letters. If yours is a sample of the modern human style, then I must say that it has at least the merit of being entertaining. However, you begin with a paragraph of the sort which one would write to someone one did not know very well and did not wish to. I am aware we do not know each other very well either, but you can afford to be natural, I promise not to be shocked or find you presumptuous. I think you must have felt that the closing sentiments were not quite right, for you were too awkward to write them in English, and I do agree with you that insincere flirtation always sounds better in French. I know it is the custom for a certain class of boy to always end a letter with such things, but I think we may dispense with it; though you may resemble both Valmont and Danceny in your various moods, I will never be like Mme de Merteuil, therefore please do not borrow their phrases! If you are not sincere, be at least original.

Having given you a lecture which would do credit even to Mama, I have only to ask you to attribute it to the natural female instinct to influence my male friends, so that you will not be disgruntled with

Your affectionate friend,
Rosaline

'Well?' Bertie peered over his shoulder. 'Really, Rupert, you should stick to the one girl, you know, or it wouldn't be - well - respectable.'

'Don't be silly, old chap, I haven't even got one girl to stick to. You can read it, if you like,' he tossed the letter to him languidly. 'I'm not quite sure what she means about my letter being amusing, though, for I did put rather a lot of effort into it. Bertie, why is it that intelligent girls always treat you like a child?'

'We are children,' laughed Bertie. 'I know what you mean, but I quite like it, because then I don't feel I have to say anything interesting or profound. Of course, I'm not a girl, and I haven't read the original letter, but it must have come across as rather eccentric, what with the insincere flirtation, as she puts it, in French and mixed in with your report, which I presume you wrote in a more normal tone. And I must say, I don't know what definitions you're referring to, but to me, it sounds like you and this girl are quite taken with each other.'

'My dear Bertie,' said Rupert patiently, 'the tone to which you refer is absolutely necessary when corresponding with vampire girls, otherwise one appears unsophisticated. I assure you, it means nothing, but a certain flavour of romanticism is required to dispel the impression, which they are likely to form automatically, that I haven't read anything: it seems to be the opinion of the vox populi that boys are illiterate.'

Bertie shook his head disapprovingly, 'Most are, old boy. Anyway, how do you know this, if you haven't had any experience?'

'Well, I'm modelling my letters on the sort of thing my father used to write, in his bachelor days. Of course, married men don't have time for writing letters, and it isn't fashionable, but Mama keeps his old letters, and I've read them. Mine is nothing compared to what he wrote, even when they were just friends: he had to resort to French for almost entire pages,' he explained.

'I must say,' said Bertie thoughtfully, 'that real vampires are much stranger than in books.'

'So are real humans, Bertie,' observed Rupert. 'There's no such thing as normal, unless it means the line which is perpendicular to the surface of a plane mirror. Now, in the light of that letter, what's your opinion on the case?'

Bertie rubbed his chin, resembling slightly a bust of Shakespeare or the dodo of Wonderland, then said gravely, 'You're the one with the opinions most times. I am completely baffled, therefore I suggest we consult the girls.'

Rupert smiled, 'Yes, you and I would have lost ourselves long ago if we hadn't consulted the girls. Let's go find them quickly, then, before any of the boys start wondering what we're doing in the dormitory at break times.'

They galloped downstairs and out into the courtyard, glancing round to see if they could find Ada and Beatrice. Rupert spotted them standing in a gaggle of other girls, who were gossiping in excited voices about something or other, while Ada listened with an expression of polite interest.

'Come on, Bertie,' Rupert pulled his reluctant friend by the arm. 'What's the matter?'

'Don't laugh at me, but there's something frightfully awkward about wandering into a crowd of girls just like that,' he replied. 'Can't we consult them later?'

Rupert suppressed a laugh, 'Really, Bertie, it's you whom Mrs Johnson should be worried about: I'm not socially awkward at all by comparison.'

'She wasn't worried about you being awkward, more about you being antisocial, which is not quite the same thing.'

'I'm not at all antisocial, you'll see!' objected Rupert, then exclaimed cheerfully to the crowd of girls, 'Hello! Nice day, isn't it?'

'Hello, Rupert,' Ada sounded relieved.

Amid intense scrutiny from the other girls, he said, feigning great anxiety, 'I say, I'm awfully worried that

I messed up the last question on the English homework. Would it be very troublesome if you showed me what you wrote?'

'Not at all; I left my things inside, but you can come with me, and I'll show you,' she smiled at the others, 'See you later!'

As they walked off, she remarked, 'I presume you don't actually need help with the English homework, but you simply want, for reasons of your own, to thwart my efforts of fathoming the mysteries of the female cliques.'

'No, indeed, but I'm sure you must have been quite bored, and anyway, I want to talk to you about our own mystery,' he replied.

'Oh, what have you found out?' she asked excitedly.

'Not much,' he admitted, 'but I wrote to Rosaline to consult her about it, and she says that it sounds like someone is interfering with your dreams, in order to block out any scenes where Isolda appears. She said she knows very little about it, but she'll do some research into dreams and write back to me.'

'Who could it be, though?' Ada wondered. 'I think it must be someone in the school, or they wouldn't know that Margaret was sending me dreams.'

'Not necessarily,' replied Rupert. 'I think these things can be done even over long distances, if one is powerful enough. But, Ada, do you think Isolda was involved in Margaret's death?'

'It does rather give that impression,' she agreed. 'I think everything would become clearer if we could talk to Margaret.'

'Yes, but we haven't seen her for some time,' he remarked. 'I think she might have been offended by the caretaker banning ghosts from the music building.'

Beatrice asked, 'I don't suppose there's a way of summoning up the spirits of the dead, Rupert?'

'You mean, like in the Odyssey?' Rupert laughed. 'I don't think I could do it: it's very difficult, I think, unless one uses dark magic, and, at any rate, can you imagine the chaos if I got caught? I don't think it would be a good idea, on the grounds of health and safety.'

'Health and safety?' echoed Bertie. 'What could go wrong? In books, this never seems to be an issue.'

'Bertie, you really shouldn't take trash fiction as an authority on magic,' he admonished. 'After all, every civilised society must have their share of bureaucracy, including health and safety, and vampires are no exception. Besides, all sorts of problems can occur if you accidentally awaken the wrong spirits because they might not want to return to their graves. No, we must try and find out as much as we can by natural means first, and then we'll see. As Inspector Bucket says, sometimes doing something just for the sake of doing it might make something else happen.'

'Perhaps,' suggested Ada, 'the teachers may be able to tell us something about her, and about what happened to Isolda after she left the school.'

The others were just agreeing to this, when the bell shrieked discordantly, being neither in tune nor in time with the chapel bells. Apparently, there had once been a time when the school and chapel bells had agreed with each other, but nobody could remember when this was.

'I'll be late for lunch, because I need to go for a selection quiz for House Challenge,' said Rupert, as they parted company.

'Indeed, that's very radical,' replied Ada. 'Usually St Anthony's are highly disorganised with House Challenge.'

'Yes, but Ernest managed to persuade Mr Jury to organise something, or rather, to put his voice of authority onto Ernest's organisation, because the current prefects are sporty and have no interest in that kind of thing. Toodle-pip!'

When lunchtime came, it occurred to Rupert that he could pursue his investigations with Mr Jury, who was always a fountain of gossip. Though he had suggested this to Bertie, the latter preferred to eat on time, and did not think he would get onto the quiz team anyway. Therefore, Rupert embarked upon his mission alone, which, he thought, was better really, as Bertie was not really necessary for the interrogation. As he climbed two flights of stairs, he smiled at the thought of impressing Ada with his findings.

Mr Jury's room was on the top floor, overlooking the courtyard. One wall was adorned with photographs of many years of school trips he had taken, scattered haphazardly among maps of the ancient world. A scholarly atmosphere presided over this room, subtly displaying itself in the vast collection of Latin texts scattered over Mr Jury's desk, which he was fond of immersing himself in when the class was being particularly dull. Perched proudly on the filing cabinet, a model Colosseum quietly gathered a respectable layer of dust. At that moment, Mr Jury was lovingly cleaning it with a spotted handkerchief, whilst Ernest leaned languidly against the wall, fiddling with his phone.

'Hello, Rupert!' he whispered enthusiastically. 'You have to be very quiet, so as not to disturb the Colosseum.'

'Ernest,' said Rupert, fixing him with a penetrating gaze, 'are you thinking of applying to be a prefect at Easter?'

He looked mildly surprised that Rupert had guessed his thoughts. 'Well, I can't make up my mind. Mr Jury thinks I should, and it would be nice, because I confess I have ambitions to win House Challenge, House Singing, et cetera. On the other hand, there's an awful lot of fussing involved, which is not optional. I'd have to speak to younger children, you know; encourage them, and all that sort of thing, but they are so very judgemental these days. And then, I would be open to being scolded by whoever the girl is; it would be like standing at a mark, with a whole army shooting at me. Rupert, be a good chap and tell me what you think.'

'I think you should do it,' he replied, 'and don't worry about the fussing and the scolding. I'm sure you can still be attractive to girls without letting them boss you around over everything.'

Ernest shrugged and smiled, then turned to Mr Jury, 'You did say start of lunch break on the notices, didn't you, sir? Everyone seems to be a bit late.'

'Hmm... yes. That's all to the good: I need a bit more time to dust the Colosseum,' he replied, with an abstracted air which descended on him whenever he thought of the grandeur of the fallen Roman empire. 'Can you believe it, boys, that Mr Mond informed me today, that Dr Botherby had been disdainful about it? He said it was just a heap of plastic, but he should look beyond the plastic, and see the greatness of Rome.'

Rupert and Ernest made sympathetic noises, and Rupert suggested, 'You could blow the dust off with a hairdryer: it might be more efficient.'

'Now, that's a very good idea, but I don't think I could pull it off without being ridiculous,' observed Mr Jury pensively. 'What do you actually want me to do, Ernest?'

'I'd just like you to ask these questions, Mr Jury,' Ernest handed him his phone.

'Really, Ernest, I don't think much of these questions,' he skimmed through them. 'I don't know half the answers myself.'

'That doesn't matter in the slightest, since you are not going to be on the team, sir. Anyhow, you know Mr Mond likes to ask obscure things about contemporary culture, so you'd hardly be expected to know the answers.'

This explanation appeared satisfactory to Mr Jury, who, in any case, was no longer listening, for the Colosseum was in danger of falling off the cabinet and disintegrating. Rupert sighed, thinking that he would hardly find out anything with this state of affairs. At that moment, the sash window suddenly opened of its own accord. Although the air had been without a murmur until this point, a strong gust of wind swept through the room, removing all the dust from the Colosseum.

'I say, how extraordinary,' observed Mr Jury. 'Did you see that, boys, how the wind blew the dust away just as we were talking about using a hairdryer?'

'Extraordinary,' Rupert agreed, smiling, then contemplated how to interrogate Mr Jury without it sounding like an interrogation.

He was just thinking that was a rather difficult thing to achieve, when Ernest complained, 'I'm very hungry now; I do wish people would turn up. It wasn't like this the year we won, but then, we had Mrs Johnson to sort things out, and it's never been the same since.'

'There are biscuits in the box underneath the second volume of the Cambridge Latin Course, if you want them,' replied Mr Jury. 'However, although I am not a touchy person, I can not help but remark upon your lack of diplomacy in implying that under my jurisdiction, St Anthony's has become, so to speak, a shambles. Although this observation is very true, you will hardly get on in life, my dear boy, unless you learn to modify and improve the truth as a matter of routine, in other words, unless you learn to be a politician. Now, I don't see why the pair of you are amused by my rare words of wisdom: the fact that I don't follow it myself proves the wisdom of the maxim.'

'Indeed, we'll bear it in mind,' said Rupert, 'but when was the last time we won House Challenge?'

'Five years ago,' he replied. 'I wasn't Housemaster then, so it wasn't such chaos as it always is now.'

'Five years ago,' repeated Rupert thoughtfully. 'Perhaps it is the ghost's restless spirit which deprives the school of its old tranquility.'

Mr Jury looked up from his biscuit, surprised, 'Ghost?' he repeated anxiously.

'Well, I don't really believe in ghosts, of course,' said Rupert lightly, 'but Mr Lloyd clearly does, hence the sign in the music building. I assumed that the only ghost the school had was Margaret, the girl who died five years ago.'

'Ah, yes,' replied Mr Jury slowly. 'Poor Margaret; she was such a sweet girl, but you know, it was a terrible scandal. Apparently, she killed herself,' he glanced around furtively, 'because she was under too much pressure, and one day she couldn't bear it any more. But I find that very strange. She was my best student that year, and she would have gone to Oxford to study Classics.'

'Did she want to go to Oxford, or did she simply have pushy parents?'

'What kind of a question is that?' he exclaimed. 'Of course she wanted to go to Oxford; everyone does, and it would have suited her perfectly. Besides, she and Isolda had offers from the same college, I can't quite remember which one now, and she was quite looking forward to being at university with her old friend.'

'You taught Isolda as well?'

'Yes, but not at A-Level. A pity really, for she was good too, though not as good as Margaret. But she did go to Oxford, studying Biology, I think,' now that Mr Jury had begun talking, the reminiscences flowed with very little input from Rupert. 'She was a strange girl, but I think she had a difficult family life, parents divorced and so forth. She never had any other friends except Margaret, but then, I don't think she ever felt the need, for she was passionately attached to her. Everyone was fond of Margaret, you know. We were all quite distraught when it happened, especially Mrs Johnson. And to think she threw herself from the tower of the castle ruins - it was so tragic, and quite out of character too, for I remember she had a fear of heights when she was younger. I shall never understand any of it, and you know, I shouldn't be talking about it to you,' he trailed off and sat gazing into a host of tragic memories.

However, the rather solemn atmosphere was soon dispelled by the start of the selection quiz, and the minor disagreement between Mr Jury and Ernest's phone. When it was over, he and Rupert hurried down to lunch, chattering about House Challenge, and Rupert felt how ephemeral and insubstantial are the memories of the dead, as he tried to puzzle out Margaret's story.

'I do wish you were a year younger, though,' Ernest was saying, 'because then you could have been a junior. There's nothing more annoying than when they don't know the answer to a perfectly easy question which we can't answer, and Mr Mond is very strict about not helping them in any way.'

'Perhaps we could impart the knowledge to them

telepathically,' suggested Rupert, half playfully half seriously, and Ernest laughed. 'Aren't we due for a rehearsal of the play soon?'

'Yes, I forced myself to schedule one for tomorrow evening,' he replied, stuffing his hands in his pockets in a disgruntled way.

'You sound quite depressed about it, and I thought it was going rather well,' said Rupert.

Ernest looked up hopefully, 'Do you really think so? No, you're just being nice; you have good taste, you can't genuinely think it's going well.'

'I say, I do believe you're still sulking because they told you that the song you wrote for Leonora was unsingable and the words were even more unintelligible than Mr Mond's original ones.'

'I'm not sulking,' he replied. 'Well, maybe the tiniest bit.'

'You know she only said that because it wasn't sufficiently in the pop style, so you ought to take it as a compliment. If you want my opinion, old chap, you should give up on the song altogether, for she won't sing it with the right expression anyway,' advised Rupert.

'And yet, I think we ought to have a song, for I get the impression that Mr Mond was proud of how poetic he managed to become in that scene,' pondered Ernest. 'I am really rather perplexed about the whole thing.'

'Well,' smiled Rupert, 'there is only one thing to be done in such dire circumstances: consult Ada.'

'She won't think I'm silly?' he asked anxiously.

'Of course not,' Rupert reassured him. 'At least, no more than she already does, but in truth, I don't think she's the slightest bit judgemental, which is most unusual for intelligent girls.'

'Or unintelligent ones,' added Ernest. 'I'll take your advice and present my problem to her at once.'

They had by this point finished their sandwiches, and, thus fortified, Ernest felt sunny and well-disposed to all the world again. He determined to persevere gallantly with the play and with this resolution, a fountain of new ideas regarding it poured forth. Meanwhile, though pleased at the high spirits of his friend, Rupert was rather wishing he had cheered him up fractionally less, as he wanted to tell Ada about his findings. As Ernest prattled on, he pondered on Mr Jury's story, shuddering involuntarily.

CHAPTER 7 - A VISIT TO THE CASTLE

As it happened, he did not have time to make his report until that evening, for by the time Ada had solved all of Ernest's problems with the play, it was time for lessons. Rupert reflected to himself that her manner of doing this was quite ingenious, and he was filled with admiration. The four of them were sitting comfortably on their usual bench by the music department, lulled by the birds blending their melodies with the miscellaneous sounds of the school. Though it was autumn, the evening was warm and the breeze gentle; now and then, a gilded leaf detached itself reluctantly from the gnarled sycamore and fluttered dreamily to the ground.

Rupert found himself gazing at her as they talked, in a way which was not usual with him. He noticed, as if for the first time, each subtle detail of her face, which appeared to him now more beautiful than before. Unconsciously, he studied the curves of her expressive mouth, the sparkling of her eyes and the way her hair rippled in the breeze - he did so, not as a lover would, but more as a young artist gazes wonderingly at a beautiful painting.

For Rupert had made up his mind quite firmly that he was not in love. It was not even the first innocent awakening of passion which leaves a boy confused and wondering, yet happier than before. Indeed, he assured himself every time he thought about her, which was most of the time, that he had no desire for anything to change. It would be foolish to mar this pure, platonic friendship by the slightest hint of something else in his feelings towards her. After all, it was out of the question that he could have a serious romance with a human girl. Having decided then, that he was not in love, he often caught himself in airy fantasies which somehow always turned to her like a compass towards north, but he was still quite content. Besides, he thought, there is nothing out of the ordinary in my appreciating her more than before, it is merely that being older, I have developed an appreciation of beauty which is more profound than before.

And yet, as he gazed at her that evening, leaning his cheek against his hand, there was an intensity in his eyes which spoke of yearning and desire and other indefinable but exquisite sensations, which were not there at all.

'So that's all I've found out,' concluded Rupert, having carefully reported his conversation with Mr Jury, accurately but without really concentrating on his own words.

'You've done extremely well,' remarked Ada warmly. 'You must not expect too many revelations at a time, especially of a more personal kind, from Mr Jury.'

'I was rather hoping she would have confided in him.'

'Rupert, if you were a girl, would you have confided your deepest thoughts to a male Latin teacher, no matter how good your relationship?'

'Oh,' said Rupert, crestfallen. 'I see what you mean,' then added, brightening up, 'However, it's quite likely that she may have confided in Mrs Johnson, as she was Housemistress of St Anthony's then, and Mr Jury implied that they had a fairly close relationship.'

'Yes, you're quite right,' Ada agreed, 'but I think you ought to leave us to probe her.'

'Of course,' said Rupert, smiling. 'I know I'm not very subtle, and the last thing we want is the teachers interfering in our investigations.'

'It is very strange,' observed Ada, 'that she, who in life was cheerful and sociable, should be so very temperamental as a ghost. It's almost as if she doesn't want to solve the case, for she has not appeared in my dreams for some time.'

'Ghosts often are a little different from the people they once were,' replied Rupert, 'and I think it is quite difficult for them to appear. Having no substance themselves, they must absorb energy from the surroundings, so their movements are usually somewhat erratic, and besides that, whoever it is who may be interfering with the dreams may also be preventing her from appearing.'

When they parted company, Rupert felt quite satisfied with the day's events, especially as Ada had praised his efforts with the case. Perhaps it was just his imagination, but at dinner she seemed to favour him with special attention, and the animation brought to her eyes by the prospect of adventure captivated and drew him to her. The evening flew by in sparkling conversation. Though he could hardly remember anything that was said - they talked of indifferent matters, for the swiftly approaching darkness made talk of ghosts seem a little too eerie - he felt that it had been unusually pleasant. As night fell over St Jude's, he fell asleep with a smile on his lips and dreamed of her.

The next morning, he was quite astonished to find a very neat paper bird nestled under his pillow. Wondering how it had got there without him noticing, he opened it at once, his heart pounding with excitement, and read:

Dear Rupert,

I can only write you a short letter tonight, for I ought not appear to be showing you too much favour - it might be misinterpreted. At any rate, the substance of my letter, though short, is rather important.

I have thoroughly perused the library at school, and have found the following relevant passage in a very dense and dusty book, entitled The History of the Vampires from the Dawn of Time to the Present Day:

'In ancient times, the art of manipulating dreams was revealed to our ancestors by the tribe known variously to history as the Dream Givers, the Dream

Explorers or the Angels of Sleep. However, it is regrettable that we have never attained such skill in it as they, nor indeed have any of the other species. This tribe, having a very small population, decided early on to integrate with the humans, so that by the middle of the 18th Century, they had all but disappeared. (For further details of their history aside from their interactions with the vampires, the reader is directed to their own literature, particularly the works of the Earl of Silverwood).'

This is the only mention which the History accords to dreams, and I have been unable to locate the books referred to in the footnote. This could be due to the high level of restriction in the school library, from which the vast majority of the Universal Vampire Library is not accessible. However, considering the high position of your parents, you may be able to access much more from your castle. I hope all this helps, and do tell me if you find out anything of interest.

Your affectionate friend,
Rosaline

P.S. Mama has discovered our correspondence - not that it was secret anyway, but she has suddenly decided to pay attention to it - and has consequently decided to inspect you more closely. Therefore, we are visiting you on the weekend. I hope this suits you; don't distress yourself and try not to make an impression which is outstanding in either direction!

Although he had perused the body of the letter

with avid interest, the post script filled him with a sense of trepidation. Indeed, the off-hand manner in which Rosaline mentioned the imminent inspection from her mother struck Rupert as very incongruous with the gravity of the situation. Drastic measures would be required to avert the impending doom.

During his reading of the letter, the school had shaken off the last vestiges of sleep, and so he was obliged to get dressed promptly and leave his reply for later. Bertie, who had seen the excited gleam in his eyes and knew by now how this was to be interpreted, could hardly restrain himself from asking questions.

As soon as they had sat down for breakfast, he demanded, 'Well, Rupert, enlighten us on the developments. What did Rosaline say?'

Rupert quoted to them the extract from the History of the Vampires and remarked, 'I'm sure I can find out more from the Universal Library, but that will have to wait until the weekend. I'm not sure when I'll get a chance to use the portal while I'm being inspected by Rosaline's mother, though. She doesn't seem to take that very seriously: I suppose she doesn't realise how formidable her mother is.'

'Don't worry, I'm sure you'll make a good impression,' Ada reassured him.

'I've just had an idea,' said Rupert suddenly. 'You three have never been to my house before; we could have an outing on the weekend, if you can get parental permission. That way, I'll be able to tell you my findings straight away, and it will allow me to escape from Lady Honoria.'

'That sounds splendid,' said Ada, 'and I'm sure my parents will agree - they are very open-minded and relaxed about everything. And I would like to meet Rosaline. What do you think, Beatrice?'

Beatrice agreed and Rupert said, 'Oh, good. I think you girls will get on very well, indeed. Bertie?'

'Yes, I'll come,' replied Bertie, setting to work conscientiously on a croissant. 'Aunt Caroline likes you, so that'll be fine, for my mother lets me do pretty much what I like anyway, and naturally Daddy doesn't even need to be considered. I wonder what my aunt would think, though, if she knew you were a vampire,' he chuckled.

'Well, that's settled then,' Rupert was pleased. 'I'll make the arrangements in Assembly,' then added, as the others looked perplexed, 'telepathically, of course.'

While Dr Botherby expounded his educational theory to the baffled students and teachers, Rupert mentally entered his mother's boudoir. His face expressed the most attentive interest in the Head of Academics' words, which merely flowed around him like the distant roar of the sea. In his mind, he saw the elegant embroidered curtains, the impressionist paintings on the white walls - his mother was somewhat modern in her taste for a vampire - and the walnut writing desk looking down onto the lake, tranquil under a grey Welsh sky. She was sitting at the desk dealing with her extensive correspondence, as was her custom in the mornings; he watched her fondly for a moment and savoured the atmosphere of the boudoir, lightly scented with roses. Sensing her son's presence in her mind, she smiled and put down the quill. The arrangements for the weekend were made and approved, then she admonished him affectionately to pay attention to Dr Botherby. When he had withdrawn his thoughts, there remained a lingering trace of him, like an echo, and she indulged a few moments in a mother's fond dreams and ambitions.

'All sorted,' said Rupert to his friends afterwards. 'Mama said she'd be delighted to have you visit and she hopes this will be conclusive evidence for Papa that I do in fact have friends. She'll arrange food, which will be perfectly acceptable to humans. I haven't bothered to tell her about the case yet, though, for I intend to present her the finished work, as it were.'

He managed later in the day to scribble down a few lines to Rosaline, to the following effect:

Dear Rosaline,

Though it is quite impossible for me not to distress myself at the thought of being inspected by your mother, who is, you must concede, a formidable lady, I look forward to seeing you with lively anticipation. I have asked Ada, Bertie and Beatrice to visit us on Saturday, so you will have a chance to discuss the dreams with Ada. Even so, I hope the presence of female company will not render me superfluous, for I intend to be very charismatic, and I shouldn't like to waste it all on your worthy parents.

I shall certainly pursue my investigations in the

Universal Library; thanks very much for suggesting it, for I was a little perplexed as to what to do next. I have, however, discovered that Margaret killed herself by throwing herself from the castle ruins, and that she had no reason to do so which anyone could have foreseen. I'll tell you more details on Saturday, but now I must conclude. Since I have assimilated your lecture most diligently, I shall forego any poetic sentiments - you can supply them yourself, if you like - and sign myself in plain, sincere English,

> Your affectionate friend,
> Rupert

Having finished this epistle, he had some slight difficulty in folding it, but he did remember to give his bird two eyes this time. Indeed, it was a much more dignified bird than his first one, but, he reflected, it would take a long time before he could be as neat as Rosaline.

No sooner had he released his messenger, than he was mildly startled by an apparition hovering beside him.

'Oh hello, Papa,' he greeted him silently, for the apparition was none other than his father. 'You know you could have just telephoned.'

'I can't abide telephones, or any human technology,' he shuddered, and almost vanished, before returning in this ethereal, silvery form. 'Anyway, it's not as if anyone else can see or hear me, and I wanted to talk without Mama listening. Apparently, Lady Honoria is visiting us again this weekend, and I understand that the cause of this is a desire to inspect you, due to the discovery of a correspondence between you and her daughter. Is this true?' he asked reproachfully.

'Yes, what of it?'

'Rupert, my dear boy, beware of the female of the species. You don't know what danger you are in by being entangled in a correspondence with Rosaline. One thing may lead to another. Lady Honoria is well aware that an alliance with our family will be socially advantageous,' his father replied significantly.

Rupert had some difficulty in not laughing, lest anyone else thought he had psychological issues, 'Oh, you needn't worry: the last line of her letter was "don't distress yourself and try not to make an impression which is outstanding in either direction." She could not have told me more plainly that I am not for her. Anyhow, I'm the one being inspected, not you; you can just talk politics to Rosaline's father, or at him, if you prefer.'

'I'd rather not. He is very tedious,' he observed haughtily.

'You are very antisocial, Papa,' remarked Rupert. 'And yet you entertain everybody else at all those political parties.'

'That's different, it's part of the job, which is why I never socialise for pleasure. I presume I don't have to talk to your school friends? Oh good, for one set of visitors is a misfortune, but two is a cataclysm,' with these ominous words, his father faded into the air.

In the event, the weekend was not nearly as cataclysmic as he had anticipated, for it turned out that Lady Honoria considered him quite superfluous, being occupied, as she was, in socialising with her friend and inspecting Rupert. The latter had a slight dilemma regarding clothes: there was, he realised a very delicate balance to be struck between not looking underdressed by vampire standards and not looking ridiculous by human ones. He brushed his silky hair and sighed at his reflection. Even in such insignificant matters, the consciousness that he was not quite right for either world obtruded itself. However, after some deliberation, he managed to solve the issue to his own satisfaction, until he discovered that Hawkins the butler had views on the subject.

'Well,' explained Rupert, 'I would feel silly in formal dress with my friends, and I would feel disapproved of in the costume of a modern teenager in front of Lady Honoria, so I settled for a compromise.'

'If you will permit me to express my opinion, Milord,' observed the butler with a shudder.

'By all means, Hawkins, but you would express it whether I wanted to listen or not,' replied Rupert.

'Well, Milord, though I understand your thoughts, the compromise merely shows you are indecisive or eccentric,' Hawkins paused before uttering the last adjective, as if anxious this would cause offence.

'Do you think so?' asked Rupert anxiously, then, throwing up his hands, announced flippantly, 'well, I don't care!'

'Milord!' cried Hawkins rebukingly. 'I am appalled.'

'Really, Hawkins, you must stop calling me that,' said Rupert. 'It's just your manner of showing your disapproval, and I know you have strong feelings about dress, but please try to restrain them. You see, if you adhere pedantically to titles, it sounds as if you're in favour of the ancien regime and inequality.'

'Milord,' said Hawkins, emphatically protruding his fangs, 'I am a butler in an aristocratic household, my father was butler here before me and his father before him. Therefore, considering my position and lineage, I do not think it reasonable that I should have to adopt an assortment of human political ideas, or change my views on dress, at a moment's notice, just because the heir develops a caprice about integration which goes below the surface.'

'It isn't a caprice,' objected Rupert indignantly. 'It's really quite usual to want to fit in with one's friends, and anyway, just because I have listened to your opinion, it doesn't make me obliged to follow it.'

'True,' conceded Hawkins. 'It is only your mother whose opinions we must all follow.'

'Of course,' smiled Rupert, pleased to have gained his point, 'and if you drop the Milord for today, I'll dress properly tomorrow, and then it won't be necessary to express your disapproval at all.'

'Very good, Rupert. Will that be all?'

'I suppose so,' sighed Rupert. 'Thank you. Oh, Hawkins, would you please tell the portraits to behave themselves, for I need all the moral support I can get to sustain the necessary manner for Lady Honoria. You know, sometimes I really don't quite know who I am: I seem to be one person at school and another at home, and at times I can't decide which is the real me and which is merely for the benefit of other people. Do you ever feel like that?'

'No, Milord,' said Hawkins, shaking his head. 'Oh, sorry, I forgot.'

Before Rupert, who, Hawkins noticed with concern, was in a confiding mood, could express any more philosophical ideas, the doorbell rang and summoned the butler away.

'That must be Lady Honoria; she is early,' he remarked.

'Oh no, I think it's Bertie, because his aunt, apparently, is well known for ringing in that Wagnerian manner,' replied Rupert. 'I'll open the door,' he added firmly. 'The fangs, you know, not to mention your general air of having walked out of the 16th Century.'

Rupert politely asked Aunt Caroline whether she would like to come in for some refreshment, but she declined, as her husband was waiting in the car. Bertie's mother could not manage without her long, and she had a great horror of Welsh weather. Rupert concurred with all her sentiments, and so secured his friend's prompt release from her disapproving gaze - not that there was much to disapprove of in Bertie, but Aunt Caroline did not like boys in general and considered it a matter of principle, just as much as voting Conservative.

'I say, it's awfully grand,' whispered Bertie with an air of reverence, slowly fixing his large eyes on the entrance hall of the castle. 'Rupert, are you in fancy dress or something?' he studied him carefully.

'No, this is a compromise,' he explained, with a pained look. 'Remember, I'm under inspection from Rosaline's mother.'

'Oh yes, I understand,' said Bertie sympathetically. 'I'm looking forward to meeting Rosaline. Is she pretty?'

'That is quite immaterial, but yes, she is pretty,' Rupert assumed an air of severity, and they both chuckled.

Presently, the girls arrived, and Rupert suggested that they have elevenses in the library. This proposition was met with universal approbation, so they all trooped into the library, followed by Hawkins with a china tea set.

'You children amuse yourselves, Hawkins will look after you,' said Rupert's mother, smiling kindly. 'I have some guests of my own who will arrive imminently, but you needn't mind them - the house is large enough for two sets of visitors.'

So saying, she discreetly left them to themselves, and a faint trace of her delicate rose perfume lingered in the air. Hawkins put the tea things down on a walnut table in the centre of the room, then also left.

'Rupert, I don't see anything to eat,' Bertie indicated the empty plates and cups, perplexed.

'Well, what would you like to eat?' asked Rupert.
'Anything at all.'

'Oh, well,' Bertie hesitated, considering, then said, 'could I have a profiterole, please?'

Rupert closed his eyes briefly and placed both

hands over a dish in the middle of the table. His friends watched eagerly, holding their breath. A moment later, an elegant pyramid of profiteroles appeared, laden with dark chocolate and cream and garnished with strawberries.

'Bon appetit!' said Rupert happily, rather enjoying his friends' expressions of admiration. 'I'll be back in a moment; I must encounter the stare of the Gorgon, and if I don't turn to stone, I shall return with Rosaline,' he assured them, as Hawkins' solemn voice in the distance announced that Lady Honoria had arrived.

'My dear, it's so lovely to see you again,' his mother was saying. 'I'm afraid I have been a little disorganised. Not being aware that you would be coming, I allowed Rupert to have his school friends round, but they won't disturb us. It is just such a pity that you won't be able to inspect him in much detail, but I do have a picture of him, which would do quite as well. Ah, here he is,' she broke off.

'Good morning, Lady Honoria,' Rupert bowed demurely, nodded politely to her husband and smiled conspiratorially at Rosaline. 'Mama has, I think, made my apologies regarding the double booking better than I could have done, but, on the positive side, I shall be nicely out of the way if you want to have profound conversations. Now, if you will permit me to abduct Rosaline to the library, I'll take my leave for the moment.'

'Well, we will see you later, Mama,' said Rosaline, before she had time to say anything. 'And you need not be concerned: Rupert will behave impeccably, and I shan't pay him too much attention, for I am anxious to experience the novelty of his friend.'

Permission was haughtily granted for this plan, and Rupert, very relieved, led Rosaline to the library.

'Well done, Rupert, I think you've struck the right balance,' she congratulated him.

'Right balance?' he echoed.

'Yes,' she replied. 'You have just enough etiquette to be approved of, and just enough boyish frivolity not to be overly liked. I suppose it came instinctively, for it is a difficult balance to calculate, but I congratulate you anyway.'

Rupert laughed, 'I must warn you, though, that Bertie is not fascinating, even if he is a novelty.'

'You should leave me to judge that for myself,' she informed him as the oak doors of the library opened themselves.

Rupert had been a little anxious that she would appear eccentric, having not had as much practice at social integration as he had, but he soon found that his fears were groundless. Indeed, Ada and Rosaline discovered within five minutes that they had much in common, and the three girls got on so well, that Rupert found himself unable to get a word in edgeways. Meanwhile, Bertie, being very accustomed to this state of affairs, philosophically did justice to the profiteroles, gazing wonderingly at Rosaline all the while and thinking that Rupert's description of her as 'pretty' was rather inadequate.

When the conversation turned to the mystery of

St Jude's, Rosaline remarked, 'I must say, you're very lucky to have such an intriguing adventure; nothing exciting ever happens in my school.'

'But it's full of vampires! Isn't that exciting?' said Bertie.

'Well, I suppose it is if you're a human,' she replied. 'We do have a few ghosts, and the pictures talk, but they always try to tell you the same stories. Portraits are so fond of hearing their own voices, like men, you know.'

At this point, a voice interrupted, 'Rupert, why do you not introduce me to your lady friends? Really, you are most inconsiderate.'

Startled, the children turned round and looked in the direction where the voice had come from. Behind them, a large picture of a hunting party hung on the oak panelled wall. However, upon closer inspection, this appeared to be no ordinary hunting party, for the horses hovered above the ground as though they were flying, and quite a few appeared to be deep in conversation with their riders. As they watched, one of the figures in the painting dismounted, flourished his hat and very deliberately repeated his remark to Rupert.

'Well, what are you staring at? Have you never seen a talking picture before?' Rupert's ancestor, for such he evidently was, gazed haughtily at Bertie.

'No, I haven't, it's most extraordinary,' murmured Bertie, somewhat abashed.

'You're unusually loquacious today,' remarked Rupert, in a tone of familiarity which surprised Bertie, for he had felt a little intimidated by the portrait's penetrating gaze.

'Indeed,' he returned affably, 'I am usually of an unsociable disposition, and I prefer to listen than to talk mostly, but you know that I am always very gallant to ladies,' here he favoured the company with a charming smile, revealing very white fangs.

Ada asked, 'Do you hear very interesting things?'

'Not usually, but the conversation has been more stimulating of late,' he observed. 'There has been much discussion about the witches. Apparently, there has been some political unrest among them again - this happens quite regularly, by the way, for the witches are a very quarrelsome group and full of radicals, not like us. However, this time we suspect it may be more serious. The Oxford League of Witches is deeply involved, I gather, but I can't stand here gossiping all day, you know. It is high time I was idling around somewhere else. Good day to you all!'

Suddenly, as if he had been caught in some forbidden act, he fell silent and froze into the canvas. He became just a small patch of paint, vibrant but lifeless.

'What is the Oxford League of Witches?' asked Ada curiously.

Rupert looked a little blank, 'I've heard it mentioned quite frequently, but I don't know much about it. There's a lot of secrecy surrounding it, you know.'

'These days, it's very mysterious,' agreed Rosaline, 'but it wasn't always like that. It's had something of a chequered history: in the Middle Ages, when witches were persecuted, it dabbled rather deeply in dark magic.'

'But how come so many witches were burned?' asked Bertie. 'You'd think they wouldn't get caught.'

'They rarely did,' explained Rosaline, 'and if they were caught, they simply feigned their own death. The unfortunate people who were burned were often not witches at all, they were merely scapegoats, for the League had become more powerful then, and it protected them from the humans. However, by Victorian times, a policy of integration had been adopted, so successfully in fact, that many influential politicians around that time were really witches in disguise, slowly conquering the humans by influence, rather than by force. For the last century, the League has been a fairly innocent organisation, a sort of club for witches who went to Oxford, its main purpose being to preserve their traditions despite their shrinking population. However, there have always been some witches who want to regain the power they have lost and conquer the world, rather than living peacefully with the other species, and, from what I gather from my parents, this group has increased in influence and is causing a dramatic split within the League of Witches.'

'Oh, it all sounds very sensational!' cried Bertie gleefully. 'It's just like a novel.'

Rupert laughed, 'I suppose it is, but if the witches really did take over the world, they would probably wipe out the humans, so this is quite important, you know, if it isn't just one of the usual false alarms. Anyway, I think it would be a good time for me to explore the Universal Vampire Library now.'

CHAPTER 8 - THE BOOK OF DREAMS

Rupert got up and walked over to the far end of the room. Curiously, Bertie followed him. As he approached the ceiling-height book case, the cumbersome leather-bound volumes suddenly opened of their own accord. They flapped around his head, fluttering their pages and creating a whirring sound like the wings of many birds. Astonished, Bertie reached out and touched one of the books, a richly illustrated edition of Gulliver's Travels. To his surprise and Rupert's amusement, the book snapped shut indignantly and shrank from his touch, so that it became small enough to have been found in Lilliput itself. Following its example, the other books also returned to their places.

'It's because your fingers still have cream on them,' explained Rupert. 'The books often seek attention from visitors, but they are very particular that they should only be touched with clean fingers.'

'Will you be long?' asked Ada.

'No,' he replied, 'you will hardly notice that I'm

gone. Time slows down drastically in the library, so you can spend weeks in there at a time, and when you come out, only an hour would have passed.'

Rupert extracted a curious signet ring from his pocket, engraved with the family arms. Inspecting the oak panels in front of him, he pressed the ring into one of the knots in the wood. After waiting a few seconds, he waved goodbye to his friends and walked straight through the wall. The panel faded momentarily, then appeared as solid as before. It was quite impossible to tell that a portal was there, and yet Rupert had vanished like mist.

Let us leave the others momentarily in the castle and follow Rupert beyond the mysterious portal. Emerging on the other side of the panel with an extraordinary sensation of lightness, he tilted his head back and gazed admiringly at the entrance hall of the Universal Vampire Library. Though he had been here a few times before, it always filled him with a sense of awe. The floor was paved in smooth marble and adorned with intricate mosaics of gems set here and there in the white stone. However, his footsteps made no more sound than those of Venus dancing on the yellow sand. Indeed, he floated above the floor rather than walking on it, and the air itself seemed not to exist, as if the whole library were hovering in some fantastical vision.

Graceful columns to the right and left reached up into the clouds, which swirled majestically overhead. In the centre of the hall, sunlight sparkled through a lofty iridescent dome, but everywhere else, the ceiling was obscured by the clouds. The hall itself seemed limitless, and all that was not touched by the golden cascade of sunlight was palled in a permanent velvety night. Yet the darkness was pleasant and welcoming, especially to a vampire's eyes. It was a soft, gentle darkness, which insidiously enveloped Rupert and lulled him into a world of dreams.

For in this place, no sound from the outside world intruded, and the sun itself hid its fire and gazed not upon the secret thoughts of those who came and lost themselves in the palace of knowledge. In the distant recesses, the only light came from the books themselves, which twinkled like keen stars. For a while - he did not know how long, as here there seemed to be no such thing as time - Rupert feasted his eyes on the scene. Elusive and sweet airs echoed around the chamber, and he strained his ears to catch them, but they always evaded him, then called him from another place. Although there were many other vampires there, he felt the most delicious solitude, for the darkness softened the otherwise obtrusive presence of company. Besides, all the rest were quite silent too, for each was listening entranced to the strange melodies which seemed to resound for him alone and echo the subtle shades of his most secret soul.

As Rupert stood there, as still as a blade of grass on those unearthly days where there is no breath of wind, his imagination soared in ecstasy, and the whole world was beautiful, and nothing was but what was not.

By and by, he became accustomed to his surroundings and considered how to begin his search. Rosaline had already looked through the ground floor and found nothing. Therefore, he must venture to the floors above, to which the access was restricted and where he had never been before. However, as far as he could see, there did not seem to be any stairs.

Just as he was pondering how to get upstairs, he observed a man in a scarlet cloak striding purposefully to the centre of the room. He stood beneath the dome with a shard of light illuminating his pale face. Rupert watched as he held his hand up to the light, so that his ring glistened with an ethereal gleam. The next moment, he soared straight up into the air and disappeared entirely.

Anxious not to lose sight of his unknown guide, Rupert hurried to imitate him. As the light struck his own ring, he was momentarily blinded. He felt the air rush past his ears, then just as suddenly, all was still. Breathless, he glanced around him. It appeared that he had successfully penetrated the next floor, and he smiled, pleased with himself. However, he was quite alone.

Suddenly, he was seized by vertigo and a terrible, aching dizziness. Everything spun confusingly, as if he were on a boat tossed by a tempest. He trembled convulsively, like a leaf in a gust of wind. Desperately, he looked for something to hold onto, for he felt himself falling. The room was entirely empty, but he seemed to be falling ever so slowly down a deep shaft, right down to the bottom of the earth, and a dark horde of goblins danced round him, grinning eerily.

Everywhere he turned, the strange shadows pursued him and gave him no peace.

After a moment, it occurred to him that his feet were still on firm ground. It was only an illusion. Yet knowing this did not stop the wild desire to scream from welling up in his throat. He bared his teeth and stared defiantly ahead of him, trying to force the illusion to dissolve.

All of a sudden, he felt normal again, and around him was only the empty library. He breathed a sigh of relief, wondering idly whose idea it was to almost scare everyone to death who entered this room. Now that the experience was over, he was a little inclined to laugh at it. Nevertheless, he now proceeded with caution, not quite knowing what to expect, and turning round apprehensively at every little sound.

This room did not have the air of vast grandeur of the entrance hall, yet it seemed to be an infinite number of rooms compressed into one. At one moment, it resembled a Gothic cathedral, at another, a bright hall lined with mirrors. Rupert was a little perplexed by all these changes, especially as he could not see any books. He carefully studied the inscriptions above the archways, or the mirrors, as they sometimes were, among many other things. In front of him was one which bore the title 'Hall of Dreams.' Beneath this, in smaller writing, Rupert read, 'Thou who art bold enough to enter here, beware, for nothing is what it seemeth.'

He contemplated this for a moment, then dismissed the ominous warning from his mind, and entered the Hall of Dreams. The door slid shut behind him with a reluctant growl. For a moment, he felt trapped, but the feeling soon passed, for he found himself in a beautiful garden. The floor turned instantly into verdant grass, speckled with wild flowers. A gentle breeze caressed his face, and the extravagantly painted ceiling melted away into an azure sky.

Rupert listened, delighted, to the harmonious birdsong and wondered what could be the meaning of the inscription when everything was so idyllic. However, the strangeness of the scene dawned on him, as he realised that what he had first taken for birds fluttering in the treetops were in fact books. Slowly, the books descended and twirled around him in a strange kind of dance. Rupert inspected the titles: they appeared to be mostly either history or works of fiction. Curiously, he opened a book at random. A radiant white light emanated from the pages, and words which he did not understand washed over him like the swelling ocean.

Overwhelmed by it all, he hastily closed the book and wandered off, followed solemnly by the other books. Suddenly, he caught sight of Ada. She was meandering ahead of him through the meadow, apparently quite unaware that he was there. He called to her, but she did not seem to hear. Surprised, Rupert ran lightly after her, but as he approached, his heart sank like lead within him: she was leaning on the arm of a strange man, gazing amorously into his eyes.

Rupert felt rather disconcerted, especially as there was something indefinably foreign about her. Yet it was definitely her. His head was in a whirl, he could only stand and stare. The strange man scooped her up in his arms. She tilted her head back and glanced briefly a Rupert, then dismissed him from her mind, as if she did not recognise him at all.

This was more than Rupert could bear. For the first time in his life, he was jealous and savagely angry. His breath stuck in his throat; despair almost suffocated him. She seemed to be separated from him by a gulf as wide as the whole world, when she lay so happily in the arms of another man. His air of possession only made it worse. A mocking smile curled over his thin lips. Triumphantly, he taunted him with the painful fact that he meant nothing to Ada. Rupert hesitated an instant between bursting into tears and hitting his rival. The strange man stared at him contemptuously. Rupert punched him.

To his utmost astonishment, his face felt remarkably soft, almost feathery. Before his very eyes, the man, who originally had been considerably taller than him, shrank in the most grotesque manner. He became very short and wide, his gait turned to waddling, and his mouth lengthened and hardened into a beak. In the space of a few seconds, he had become a pigeon. Of Ada, there was not a trace. The pigeon cocked its head on one side, fixed Rupert with a beady eye, then flapped off with comical dignity.

This extraordinary metamorphosis left Rupert quite speechless for a moment. The words inscribed above the door echoed in his head, for now he understood their meaning. Nothing around him was real;

it was all in his imagination. He chuckled to himself, feeling light-hearted all of a sudden, as he reflected that this figment of his erratic mind, whom he had been so furious with, in fact made rather a nice pigeon. However, the whole experience had made him feel emotionally drained, and he was beginning to see the most ridiculous things. Perhaps Mr Mond's conviction that he had psychological issues was not completely unfounded!

Rupert scanned the hall anxiously, but the door through which he had entered had vanished. He circled the room, methodically inspecting it for some other door, which was not the easiest task when his surroundings kept changing so capriciously. For the first time, he became aware of the strange workings of his subconscious, as if he were in a waking dream. This was an interesting, though not altogether pleasant experience, for his opinion of himself as a very reasonable and normal person was constantly being refuted by these visions. The second time he went round, Rupert noticed a low, carved door in the darkest recess of the room. This had certainly not been there before, but he was by now quite accustomed to nothing remaining the same for very long, so he thought nothing of it.

Without hesitating an instant, Rupert hastened through the door. A steep, stone staircase wound upwards in front of him. Quickly, Rupert climbed the spiral staircase and found himself in a round turret. The room was very bare and sombre, the only things in it being a heavy book bound in leather on an ornate pedestal, and a chair with claws for feet in front of it. On this chair was seated an elegant lady, past the blossom of youth but still graceful. What made Rupert start was that she had vermillion eyes.

For a moment, Rupert and the dragon inspected each other. She appeared to consider him with mild curiosity, whilst he shifted awkwardly on his feet, wondering what was the best way of addressing a dragon. Everything he had read about them flitted through his mind chaotically, and he was not encouraged by the vague impression of something he had heard, to the effect that female dragons were especially formidable. However, retreat was out of the question. The dragon having appeared in the guise of a lady, Rupert blushed up to his eyes, suddenly realising that he must seem very ill-mannered.

'Good morning, Madame,' he said, with a charming smile. 'I hope I am not disturbing you.'

'No, indeed,' returned the dragon, in an amiable tone, though her voice did resemble the distant rumbling of thunder. 'My solitude is so rarely interrupted up here that I am always glad of company. There is something rather familiar about you, which makes me fancy I have seen you before,' she pondered.

'No, this is the first time I've been here,' he replied. 'I am sure I should never forget the pleasure of making your acquaintance,' he added suavely.

'Ah, now I know who you are; it's Rupert, isn't it? You are every inch your father's son. He has just that same expression when he's trying to be gallant,' she chuckled, a laugh which sounded like crackling flames.

'I didn't know you knew my father,' he said, surprised.

'My dear child, I know everybody who is anybody,' she replied condescendingly. 'I may be getting middle-aged, but all the influential vampires still say to each other: we are in a difficult situation, therefore let us consult Lady Gwendolen. However, public figures these days are very tedious, with the exception of your parents. Things were so different, when I danced as a young girl at your castle,' she sighed nostalgically.

'I am frequently informed,' Rupert ventured to observe, 'that the general state of society is much better now than in past centuries.'

'The humans are certainly a little less barbaric than they used to be, in Wales at least,' she agreed. 'My opinion is that they will continue to be a primitive and uncultured race so long as men are in charge of everything. However, humans did not obtrude themselves on our attention so much in the past, so I certainly felt that society was more refined. You are much too young to remember, so it is good that you can find something to appreciate in the modern age, I suppose,' she remarked dubiously.

'Oh, I find modern architecture rather ugly, and I have never been able to use computers effectively without the assistance of magic, but apart from that, I enjoy St Jude's very much indeed,' he replied innocently.

Lady Gwendolen gazed at him with her piercing red eyes, 'How old are you?' she asked severely.

'Fourteen. Is something the matter?'

'Yes and no,' she replied. 'I suspect there will be a fuss when a librarian finds you, because you should not be able to get up here at all until you come of age, and most vampires don't succeed on their first attempt then. However, since you are here, you might as well stay.'

'Do you mean that all those illusions were meant to keep me out?'

'Yes, of course. You appear rather indignant,' she smiled.

'Well, it was very unpleasant,' began Rupert.

'I imagine it must have been unpleasant, especially having your beloved stolen from you by a grotesque man. I am not sure what the pigeon signified, though.'

Rupert looked appalled, 'Oh dear, I rather wish you hadn't seen that; it makes me feel rather silly.'

'Well, you could have turned back. The door would have appeared if you had really wanted it to.'

'No, I couldn't possibly turn back,' he said decisively. 'Do you observe everybody's visions in that room?'

'Yes, they are rather entertaining, and there is endless variation, for the Hall of Dreams always reflects the psychology of whoever enters it.'

'My psychology isn't like that at all!' he protested. 'That was much more along the lines of Heinrich Heine.'

'Rupert, do not presume to understand yourself at your tender age,' Lady Gwendolen admonished, in a manner which would have been like an aunt, had she not been a dragon. 'Most men take at least two centuries to understand themselves, let alone anyone else. By the way, why did you want to come here?'

'Well, that's rather a long story,' explained Rupert, 'but the crux of the matter is that I need to consult the literature of the Dream Givers, and, not being able to find anything in the entrance hall, I decided to explore.'

'In that case, you had better consult the Book of Dreams,' she advised him, indicating the volume on the pedestal. 'This is the most comprehensive treatise on their art, but I doubt you'll be able to make much sense of it: for one thing, it is all written in Latin.'

'That's no problem,' he reassured her. 'Mama has ensured that I've had a classical education.'

'Indeed, I am pleased to hear that your human education has not made you entirely ignorant,' she remarked with an air of slight disapproval. 'However, even if you do understand the words, you will be unable to comprehend their meaning, which is almost always unintelligible to those outside their tribe: as I suppose befits a people who deal with dreams, they are in general very abstract in their thoughts and writings.'

'Never mind,' said Rupert, although he felt a little discouraged. 'I'll make a copy, and worry about understanding it later.'

He took an unusually thick piece of parchment from his pocket and placed it over the first page of the Book of Dreams. Pressing the stone of the ring into the paper, he watched as a perfect copy appeared almost instantly. Quickly, he turned the page and continued copying in the same manner, a little anxious lest he be found and turned out before he had got very far. Indeed, it was a remarkably thick volume, and after a while he began to sense that his parchment was growing tired.

'You won't be able to copy the whole thing in one go,' observed Lady Gwendolen. 'I'm quite impressed at your getting so far already, for being of a complicated nature, this book in particular usually causes difficulties. Why do you wish to consult the Book of Dreams anyway?' she asked, as Rupert continued with his copying.

He explained to her at length how he and Ada had first encountered the ghost in the music department, how she had tried to communicate with Ada in dreams and how she had now fallen silent, as though she were afraid to appear. The dragon listened attentively, as he told her all he had gleaned from Ernest and Mr Jury about Margaret's story, and the mysterious part which Isolda played in it.

However, before she could express her opinions on the subject, they were suddenly interrupted by the unwelcome arrival of a junior librarian. This individual was of a somewhat grotesque appearance, being rather short for a vampire yet having an air of great majesty and importance. His ears were the most noticeable part of him, as they waggled in a most comical manner almost continuously, expressing his great agitation and disapproval.

'How did you get here?' he demanded of Rupert, rather crossly. 'You haven't got a pass!'

'Yes, I have,' said Rupert, presenting his ring for inspection.

The librarian carefully looked at it from all angles, then sighed, shaking his head in exasperation, 'Really, of all the irresponsible parents in Britain, your father is the worst: he's given you his pass, without restrictions!'

'Well, there's no need to get upset about it,' remarked Rupert. 'Nothing disturbing has happened at all.'

'That's just what I can't understand,' replied the librarian in a disgruntled tone, as if he rather wished that something had happened. 'You should have fainted in the antechamber. Didn't you begin to feel dizzy, as if you were falling a very long way into deep darkness?' he asked anxiously.

'Oh yes,' said Rupert, 'and there were goblins too, but then I realised it wasn't real, so I felt quite well again.'

'Oh dear, oh dear, how dreadful!' the librarian wrung his hands. 'I shall have to report this. Lady Gwendolen,' he turned reproachfully to the dragon, 'why did you not inform me at once that he had penetrated to the turret?'

'I did not think it was a matter of much consequence,' she replied haughtily.

'Not a matter of consequence!' he cried indignantly. 'The security must be tightened. If boys of fourteen are able to wander upstairs freely, wantonly, as it were, it will be the end of civilisation as we know it!'

'There isn't actually an age limit,' objected Lady Gwendolen. 'Although it is highly unusual for a small boy's magical powers to be sufficiently developed in order to get past security, I do not think it is necessary to make a fuss in these unusual cases - we must not discriminate against small boys, you know,' she added in a tone of great political correctness, before indicating to the librarian that the conversation was at an end by breathing smoke on him.

Rupert smiled gratefully at the dragon. Though not exactly pleased at being referred to as a small boy in that manner, he was sufficiently astute to gather that she was conferring upon him a mark of great favour. He decided that it would be sensible to submit to being turned out by the officious librarian, to avoid any more fuss. Besides, he had a copy of a considerable proportion of the Book of Dreams, and he could always come back for more if necessary. For it never even occurred to him that the tightened security might keep him out.

'Now, you had better come along with me, young man,' said the librarian with severity. 'I shall have to reprimand your father.'

'Right-ho,' Rupert acquiesced politely.

'I'm surprised your mother hasn't already done so,' he continued.

'Probably she had better things to do,' he replied.

'What were you doing there anyway? I don't see what you could possibly want with that book.'

'The reasons for which I require to consult the

Book of Dreams are entirely private and confidential, I'm afraid,' Rupert remarked, drawing himself up and looking so much like his father that the librarian was taken aback.

'I see,' he responded laconically.

At this juncture, Lady Gwendolen decided she had had quite enough company for one day and precipitated their departure by surrounding them with a circle of flames. In another moment, they were whisked away in a whirlwind of flickering lights and ended up back in the castle library, to the great astonishment of the other children.

Hawkins, sensing the presence of a stranger in the castle, bustled in and said, in his most ceremonious voice, 'Good day, sir, how may I help you?'

'I must speak with the duke at once.'

'Their Graces have visitors and are at present engaged.'

'You mean the duchess has visitors, so the duke can be spared,' insisted the librarian.

In response to an inquiring look from the butler, Rupert put in, 'Really, Hawkins, there's no need to be alarmed, though I'm sure Papa would like an excuse to escape from Lady Honoria. All that happened was that I was discovered by this er... gentleman in the turret of the Hall of Dreams, and he wishes to complain about it.'

'Very well, I shall fetch him,' Hawkins replied and left.

'Oh dear, what a lot of bother over nothing,' complained Rupert, sinking into a chair.

'Don't be distressed,' Rosaline reassured him. 'You know, I was just wondering whether you'd made an excessively good impression on my mother by not being there to exhibit any follies, but this incident will tip the balance so that you'll be quite safe.'

'Well, what did you find out?' demanded Bertie.

Rupert glanced at the librarian, then replied emphatically, 'My dear chap, it is private and confidential. I will reveal everything in school; here is too public.'

Before Bertie could reply to this, Rupert's father entered the library languidly and uttered the usual commonplace remarks very politely, wondering at the same time what the fuss was about now. The librarian made his complaint with great pomposity, and he listened, nodding to indicate beyond doubt that he was in fact listening. Meanwhile, he exchanged a knowing smile with his son.

'Really, your Grace, I am aware that you are very busy, but you must take a little responsibility. What is to become of the library if teenage boys are loose in the upper floors?'

'I quite understand and agree with you,' replied Rupert's father seriously, somewhat to the surprise of the librarian. 'However, let us not exaggerate the situation: Rupert is only one teenage boy, and I am sure he can't do much harm single-handedly.'

'Certainly, but you will restrict his access from now on, will you not?'

'Of course, of course, as soon as I have time. Will you take some tea? No? Well, it's been a pleasure. Farewell.'

When the librarian had taken his leave, he returned the ring to Rupert, remarking, 'Well, you've had your first experience of how backwards and closed-minded the librarians can be.'

'Aren't you going to restrict it, like he said?'

'No,' replied his father, smiling. 'I don't think there would be much point. Just try not to get found next time.'

'Thank you, Papa,' said Rupert. 'Anyway, Lady Gwendolen said it wasn't actually prohibited.'

'That's all fine then. The ladies must always have the last word, especially if they are dragons. I don't know what you're up to, Rupert, but I shan't bother to interfere, as I imagine it's...'

'Private and confidential!' concluded Bertie.

'Precisely!' laughed Rupert's father. 'Right, I must get back to the formidable Lady Honoria and her tedious husband.'

When he had gone, the others gathered excitedly around Rupert and asked what had happened. They listened, enraptured, as he described to them the Hall of Dreams and his strange and beautiful visions. Unlike most boys his age, Rupert was very good at telling stories, even narrating the events in the correct order. However, he felt it was best to omit the details of his experience regarding the strange man who was metamorphosed into a pigeon. When he had finished, they all leaned forwards and peered eagerly at the thick, creamy pages of the Book of Dreams. For a moment, they preserved a reverent silence, as was quite proper to the occasion, looking intently at the close black writing which crawled all over the page, full of swirls and curlicues.

'Well, I don't see this being much use: it's all in Latin,' Bertie observed, rather superfluously.

Rupert frowned slightly as he studied it, 'I understand the first bit, which just seems to be history and a general sort of introduction,' he turned the page, 'but after that it becomes very confusing. There are words, phrases, even sentences of which I know the meaning, yet they seem to bear no relation to each other. Here, for instance: a ship... a garden where the rain weeps onto beautiful roses... the moon covering the sun... I suppose that means an eclipse... a corpse that walks at night. With all of that in one paragraph, along with other words I don't recognise, I haven't the slightest idea what it means.'

'Perhaps we could ask Mr Jury about it,' suggested Beatrice. 'You could just tell him you found it lying around in the castle, to avoid suspicion.'

'I doubt your teacher would be any help,' Rosaline remarked. 'You see, this is no ordinary book, and to understand it, one must look beyond the superficial meaning of the words. In old books of magic, the words themselves often appear to be nonsense, unless one has a deeper understanding.'

Ada looked at it curiously, and for a moment the ink swam and merged before her eyes into something else.

'Well, what do you think?' inquired Bertie, breaking the spell.

'I'm not sure yet,' she replied, 'but somehow I feel it

is speaking to me, and I reach out to it, but then everything becomes obscured. It's rather like Alice in Wonderland, don't you see? All those things Rupert read out are fairly ordinary in the right context - even the thing about the corpse, in the context of a ghost story - but they are all merged together, apparently without sense, the way reality is merged in dreams. But dreams never seem to be irrational while you are in them, and I feel this book is like that, in the sense that one must look at it with the eyes of a dreamer. You don't think I'm mad, do you? You do understand?'

The others all looked at each other, perplexed, then Rosaline said, 'No, I don't understand, but I can imagine. When I look at this book, I see nothing, because it is not speaking to me. The thing about books of magic is that they almost have minds of their own. You have to be on the same energy level as them, and you don't read them like an ordinary book: instead, they speak to you.'

'Yes,' chimed in Rupert, 'you explained that much better than I could have, and that's why there are some vampire books which only we can read. It takes time though, for your spirit to be sufficiently awakened, so there are some which are all Greek to me, even if they are written in English, as the more modern ones are. The strange thing is, there seems to be a connection forming between you and the book, Ada.'

'Definitely,' agreed Rosaline. 'It all fits, as well, with those dreams you were having. It is, as it were, a spiritual awakening.'

'But I don't understand it,' said Ada, flustered but

intrigued. 'I am completely normal. There's nothing supernatural at all in my family, I'm quite certain.'

'It is possible that it has been hidden for several generations,' explained Rosaline. 'However long it has remained concealed, the blood always comes out in the end. You don't need to be alarmed about it,' she added comfortingly. 'Nothing will change unless you want it to. Just wait and see.'

Ada nodded and smiled gratefully. She was not quite sure what to think about all this: it was rather exciting, like something that might happen in a novel, but a part of her shied away from the great unknown. Then her gaze fell on the book again, as if drawn to it, and the voice urging her to remain in the refuge of normality promptly melted away.

'Rupert,' she turned her luminous eyes on him gravely, 'I feel drawn to this book irresistibly. May I have the copy for a little while?'

'Of course,' he replied. 'Let it rest until Monday, then I'll bring it to school. I have an instinct that it will reveal something important to us when the time is ripe.'

This significant remark seemed to naturally draw the curtain over the subject for the moment, and the rest of the day was spent in an almost ordinary manner, all things considered. However, the air of vague dissatisfaction with which he had greeted Hawkins in the morning had been replaced by an irresistible desire to smile at everything, as he thought of the great adventure that they were on the verge of together.

CHAPTER 9 - THE RUBY IN THE SKY

When they returned to school on Monday, St Jude's seemed disappointingly ordinary after the enchantment of the weekend. Even the castle ruins seemed peacefully oblivious to any tragedy haunting their crumbling walls, encrusted with moss and lichen. Rupert had secretly given Ada the book as soon as they arrived, but she barely had time to glance at it, and the voice which she had heard in the castle was silenced by the bustle of the school. Margaret made no further appearances either, so that it was almost as if she had never existed. However, there was always so much to do - choir, orchestra, rehearsals of Mr Mond's play - and the children immersed themselves in the small pleasures of school life with enthusiasm.

Indeed, the play had rather taken over, with rehearsals crammed into every possible corner of the day, much to the gratification of Mr Mond and the increasing distress of Ernest. Since they were in different houses, Rupert did not see much of Ada during all these rehearsals, but he concluded that hers were much more successful than his, from their discussions on the subject. The boys unanimously attributed this to the remarkable organisation of Mrs Johnson. Meanwhile, Mr Jury had retreated from the overwhelming demands of crowd control, so that, in the words of a perturbed Ernest, he 'just sat there like his grandfather carved in alabaster.'

'You can't possibly conceive how dreadful these rehearsals are,' he complained. 'Mr Jury is only there as a sort of figurehead representing organisation, whilst I, the living embodiment of chaos, attempt to say something constructive over all the noise.'

He was making these remarks on the Wednesday at lunchtime, by which it may be inferred that his resolution made on the Monday to rehearse every day would soon be broken. Indeed, the stress which the Lilliputians caused him was made plain by an involuntary tightening of the mouth whenever he spied one on the horizon. Fortunately, the bass section of the school choir provided a brief sanctuary, from which he told the tale of his woes to his younger friends.

'That does sound very stressful,' said Ada sympathetically. 'However, perhaps you are just trying too hard.'

Ernest sighed, then laughed at himself good-humouredly, 'No, indeed, I'm not trying nearly as hard as I was to begin with. Originally, I actually wanted people to listen to what I was saying, but I quickly realised that trying to shout over the din only spoiled my singing voice. So now I just talk without worrying about whether anyone can hear me.'

'All things considered, it's not going too badly,' remarked Bertie optimistically. 'At least we can get through the first act without anyone forgetting their lines.'

'That is true,' replied Ernest, 'and even though I feel some of the younger children are putting all the wrong expression in, hopefully careful direction will at least make them comical, if not correct. By the way, I've been studying Act Four carefully, and I really think it's the best bit. Mr Mond managed to get the school legend in too.'

'What school legend?' asked Rupert curiously.

'Have you not heard it before? Well, I will tell you,' replied Ernest, folding his hands and pausing with the air of someone about to say something of great interest. 'The school was once the site of an ancient fortress, the ruins of which you can still see at the castle gate. It has been the site of much bloodshed and sorrow, as well as of much romance, if the stories are to be believed. Several hundred years ago, there was a lord of the castle, who married a beautiful young woman of dubious parentage. This caused great surprise among the aristocracy, especially as he had been obstinately single for many years. However, he was quite mad with love for this girl; she became an obsession for him and he married her in spite of all opposition. I've forgotten what his name was, but hers was Isolda. Anyway, people began to suspect strange things of the Lady Isolda, and gradually rumour spread that she was a witch. These rumours did not disturb the happy couple, for she appeared to be the very soul of innocence, and he was only her humble worshipper. All was well, until the husband introduced his friend from childhood to her, and she became afflicted with passion for him. Mr Mond adds a great many details to this part of the story, but I will come to the point. One night, the husband, tormented by jealousy and suspicion, saw Isolda going to meet her lover. He followed, and when it was quite beyond doubt that she was unfaithful, he revealed himself to the startled couple. Furious, he killed his wife's lover, who had been his friend. As for her, he imprisoned her in the tower of the castle, where she pined and wasted away. The curious thing was, that since this incident, the lord lived as a cursed man. He shunned all company, misfortune fell upon all connected with him, and he himself went mad and died soon after his lady, who fell grievously ill so suddenly and unexpectedly that it was almost as if she had been cursed herself. One of this man's idiosyncrasies was, that after the death of Isolda, for whom all his love had turned to bitter hatred, he made a point of carrying her miniature about with him. The legend claims that she was in fact a witch, and that her spirit lived on in her portrait, which though long lost, still perpetuates her curse upon all her husband's dynasty.'

As Ernest finished his story, the children were joined by Mrs Johnson and Miss Gourlay. The former, having decided to take the young biology teacher under her wing, wished to introduce her to the choir, of which she had for many years been a member. Miss Gourlay herself was fond of music, as well as being keen to witness the phenomenon of Mr Finchby's conducting.

'Hello everybody,' Mrs Johnson beamed cheerfully at her students. 'How come you are telling them the school legend, Ernest?'

'I have discovered that Mr Mond has borrowed it for his play, with embellishments, of course,' replied Ernest.'

'Ah yes, Mr Mond has a very lively imagination.'

'What embellishments did he put in?' asked Ada.

'Well, as I said, he makes the most of Lady Isolda's adultery, which takes up many lines of his version, being the most fascinating part, I suppose.'

'Ernest!' admonished Mrs Johnson. 'Don't be improper!'

'I'm sorry,' he replied meekly. 'Anyway, Mr Mond has her giving birth to an illegitimate child during her imprisonment. She gives this long soliloquy, cursing her husband, lamenting her lover and then decreeing that one day her descendant will find her miniature and unlock her soul, so that she may never perish, but that her revenge may be eternal. At the end of this speech, she very dramatically dies.'

'Gosh, that sounds dark,' remarked Bertie. 'I'm not sure how it's relevant to the rest of the plot, though.'

'Well, it's not relevant at all really, except that he attributes the seduction of Lady Isolda to the errant knight Sir Jeremy,'

'So does Jeremy die?' asked Bertie hopefully.

'Yes, but then he gets resurrected in the fifth act,' explained Ernest. 'Mr Mond did have one rather ingenious idea though: he did actually have a couple of scenes where Isolda's descendant - conveniently referred to as Isolda II - searches for the miniature. However, the strange thing is, he changes the subject right in the middle of the most exciting bit, when she's performing a spell of some sort to awaken the spirit. It was as if he had completely forgotten to finish the story, which was such a pity, for this was much more sensational than all the rest of the play. What do you think, Rupert?'

However, Rupert did not register this question, as he seemed to be lost in thought. It had suddenly occurred to him that there was something uncanny about the coincidence of the witch being called Isolda. He had stopped paying much attention to Ernest when he came to the end of his speech, for he noticed that Miss Gourlay seemed startled by the mention of the second Isolda. The change was so subtle, and it was gone in an instant, that it could easily have been his imagination. Yet he was quite sure that it meant something, though he could not say why.

'Rupert?' persisted Ernest.

'Oh yes, absolutely!' he agreed promptly.

'I spoke to Mr Mond about it too,' said Ernest.

'I hope you did not offend him by telling him that you found his play erratic and illogical,' put in Mrs Johnson.

'Oh, of course not. He was flattered by my interest, and he said that he had an idea for the end of the story of the witch's descendant. He said it involved a murder, but as he was about to write it, the phone rang, and when he came back, the idea had vanished. He's still trying to find it.'

Before anyone could comment on this revelation, Mr Finchby attacked his music stand with his baton and commanded the choir to be silent. They then proceeded to stumble their way through the Bach Magnificat, with Mr Finchby becoming increasingly distressed and irate. All the way through the rehearsal, Rupert puzzled over the story of the witch Isolda, but could make nothing of it. He became so preoccupied that he started singing the soprano line by mistake, and only realised when Bertie had prodded him emphatically. Although he tried to look at Ada from time to time, they were too far apart to hold communication with their eyes. Besides, she appeared completely absorbed, either in the music - which was unlikely, as it was going very out of tune - or in her own thoughts.

At the conclusion of the rehearsal, the Director of Music bustled off, leaving the choir to mill around and chat freely once more. Rupert glided at once through the crowd to find the girls, who were talking to Mrs Johnson and Ernest about the play.

'By the way, Ernest,' added Mrs Johnson, 'Miss Gourlay has kindly agreed to run an Oxbridge entrance exams class, on Friday, isn't it?'

'Yes, I thought some of the Sixth Form might be interested,' she smiled.

'Oh yes! I have always wanted to go to Oxford, and it will give me an excuse not to attend my own rehearsal.' cried Ernest gaily, despite Mrs Johnson shaking her head at the indiscretion of this last remark.

Rupert began to listen attentively, feeling that this was a much more interesting conversation than at first appeared, but Ada warned him with a look not to betray any emotion. He put his hands into his blazer pockets carelessly and adopted his listening expression.

'I didn't know you had been to Oxbridge, Miss Gourlay,' remarked Ada pleasantly. 'I know it's quite early to be thinking about university, but I am very interested in Oxford. Which college did you go to?'

'Urganda College, Oxford,' she replied. 'It is a small and quite ancient one, which is not very well known, but I think you would enjoy it very much: it is very musical.'

'Indeed, I had not heard of it before,' continued Ada, 'but I think a small college has a lovely air of intimacy which I would like very much. Is there a choir, by any chance?'

'Oh yes, the choir is very good. I was a choral scholar myself, for I had been to a church school and I enjoy singing very much,' she smiled nostalgically.

Mrs Johnson interrupted, 'I think it is time we all got to lessons.'

'Yes, of course,' Miss Gourlay agreed, looking slightly startled to be dragged abruptly from her memories. 'Come and chat to me about university and your plans whenever you like, my dear,' she added kindly to Ada.

When they had left and the children were hurrying

to lessons, Rupert contemplated what he had heard. He felt instinctively that there was something significant in this conversation, something mysterious about Miss Gourlay which he had never noticed before. It was not until after prep that a thread emerged between little incidents in his mind.

'This may all seem a bit far-fetched,' he began at dinner, 'but don't you think it's rather a strange coincidence that the witch of the school legend was called Isolda?'

'Do you mean that the story could be true, that her descendant returned here to find her miniature, and that was our Isolda?' asked Beatrice excitedly. 'It does seem a little unrealistic, though.'

'I know it sounds like something in a novel, but it is quite possible,' replied Rupert. 'It is very common in old witch families to have a traditional name which is passed down through many centuries. It was just an idea.'

'We haven't really got any other clues, anyway,' remarked Bertie, 'unless Margaret decides to appear again.'

Ada remarked pensively, 'Rupert, did you notice that Miss Gourlay seemed very slightly startled when she came in and Ernest was telling the story?'

'Yes, I did,' he agreed enthusiastically. 'I can't explain why, though. By the way, you seemed preoccupied in choir.'

'I was standing directly in front of Miss Gourlay, so I could hear her quite distinctly,' explained Ada. 'Her singing voice is quite unique; you couldn't really mistake it, but I felt like I had heard it before, even though this was the first time I have heard her sing.'

'That is curious,' replied Rupert. 'I was just wondering if perhaps she might be related to Isolda - a cousin or something. Which would explain why she was startled by the mention of her name, even though it was in a completely different context. The other reason that this occurred to me was that she was a chorister herself and studied biology at Oxford as well.'

'The college she was at has a strange name,' observed Bertie. 'They're normally named after saints or something religious, aren't they?'

'Yes, I don't think I've even heard of Urganda College before,' agreed Beatrice.

'I have,' said Rupert. 'I'm just trying to remember where.'

Ada laughed, 'Whoever named it must have been rather eccentric. The only context in which I have heard the name is in Don Quixote.'

'Of course!' cried Rupert. 'Don Quixote goes on about a powerful sorceress called Urganda the Unknowable.'

'You are telling me that an Oxford College was named after a fictional witch. Really, Rupert?' Bertie stared at his friend in disbelief.

'She was a real witch,' replied Rupert. 'The college is named after her and it is at the heart of the Oxford League of Witches. That's why the name was familiar to me.'

'I don't think Miss Gourlay could be a witch,' Bertie observed dubiously.

'Well, obviously normal people go there too, it's just that a lot of witches do as well. I don't think Miss Gourlay is a witch either, in spite of her name.'

'Is that a common witch name?' asked Beatrice.

'Yes, especially in Scotland,' he replied.

'Like that strange old woman, Ailsie Gourlay, in Scott's Bride of Lammermoor, do you mean?' chimed in Ada.

'Precisely. When it comes to the supernatural, old novels often contain a grain of truth,' Rupert nibbled his sponge cake thoughtfully. 'I wish we could find out something about Isolda, for there's not much else we can do.'

'Perhaps we can glean something from school records and gradually build up a picture of her life that way,' suggested Ada. 'Perhaps the truth is right before our eyes and we are just not looking in the right way. I'm sure we can find her, and she may be able to tell us about Margaret's death, for she can't have just disappeared off the face of the Earth after leaving St Jude's.'

The others all agreed that this was the best thing they could do at that moment, and they did not discuss the case further that evening. However, Ada was still thinking about it constantly. When it was time to go to bed, she still felt wide awake. She did not think she would be able to sleep until she had discovered something. As the whispering in the dormitory subsided and sleep stole softly over the other girls, a feeling of impatient excitement pervaded her whole being.

At last - everyone being fast asleep by now - she

carefully extracted the Book of Dreams from under the mattress. A frail sliver of moonlight crept through a chink in the curtains, but no stars peeped through the veil of darkness which shrouded the school. However, although the wan moon was not bright enough to illuminate the book, she could see the words as clearly as if it were broad daylight. The pages themselves glowed with a soft, golden light. They were warm to touch, and smelled of summer.

If she listened very closely to the rustling of the pages, she could hear the most beautiful music. A shudder of excitement and wonder pulsated through her, for she felt that there was enchantment at her fingertips. A melodious voice emerged out of the music, and she listened more intently. It was whispering to her mysteriously, telling her to close her eyes and listen.

'Ada, open your mind to me,' it murmured. 'Listen to my voice resounding, let it wash over you like the waves of the boundless ocean; close your eyes, forget everything and let me take you into the land of dreams.'

Gradually, the dormitory faded away into obscurity. The darkness enveloped her, and she could hear the lapping of waves and the whistling of the wind. After a few moments, a bright point emerged on the horizon. She was drifting slowly towards the light, which grew and flooded the darkness.

'You can open your eyes now,' said the voice gently.

When she did, she found herself all alone on a headland with no sign of human life for miles around.

Seagulls wheeled through the air and skimmed the surface of the sea, shrieking gleefully to each other. The grass rustled in a mild breeze, but she could not feel it beneath her feet. Sight, sound and smell were all more vivid than in real life, but the sense of touch had disappeared, so that she walked as if on air.

She felt the presence of the voice beside her, but nothing broke the sepulchral solitude. When she felt a touch on her arm, she was startled, but the voice reassured her. Now she could hear it clearly, she registered that it was a man's voice, low but very soft and caressing, and full of depth like the ocean. By some unaccountable prejudice, she assumed that, though invisible, the possessor of such a voice must be as handsome as a god.

'Ah, it has been such a long time, Ada,' he observed, 'since I last spoke to anyone, that I have been quite lonely. Of course, there is always the book, my magnum opus, but over the centuries I have grown a little bored even of my own work.'

'Who are you?' asked Ada curiously.

'I was a prince of the Dream Givers, many centuries ago, but now I am merely a voice, an insubstantial spirit residing between the pages of a book,' he sighed with a gentle melancholy. 'Ovid was mistaken when he said that a poet's life is lengthened everlastingly by fame, for now there are very few people who have even heard of the Book of Dreams, let alone read it, and poor Prince Geoffrey is as forgotten as the dying leaves each autumn. Who would have thought it, Ada, considering I had such a reputation among our people in my youth? But that is the way of the world, and my brief candle has been out so long that I am quite resigned to it, though I did get a little offended when some foolish historian discovered me in the dreary records of time and confused me with a human named Geoffrey of Monmouth! Even though I was around about five hundred years before him!'

'Were you alive then, in the time of King Arthur?' asked Ada, intrigued. 'Is Geoffrey of Monmouth's Historia true?'

'Well, I had only just died quite recently before Arthur became king, so I still took a lively interest in worldly affairs. However, I can confirm that the Historia is mostly accurate, for I had a little input in it myself: it was I who communicated the Merlin prophecies to him through dreams, even though the original manuscript had long been lost. However, I had to let him embellish it a bit and put in some dates which I could not quite remember, in order to make it authoritative enough to be accepted by the Oxford scholars. He was my first pupil, if I remember rightly, and I suppose that is why we have occasionally been mixed up, since we also have the same first name. He has not been forgotten yet, though he has been ridiculed by the ignorant humans ever afterwards, which is worse.'

'Have you had many pupils?' Ada eventually managed to get a word into the monologue of the loquacious prince.

'Only a few, which is why I like to talk a lot when I do find one, as I never know how long I might be alone for afterwards,' Geoffrey replied. 'You see, with Geoffrey of Monmouth it was easy, for he was only half a human - his mother was one the Dream Givers. However, since then, we have gradually integrated with the humans so successfully that the gift has been lost for the most part, so I rarely make the effort to impart my wisdom. My last contact was Sigmund Freud, but I do not like to claim him as a pupil: we did not get on very well, because he had a dreadful habit of trying to analyse me. I do not like to be analysed; therefore, I promptly retreated back into the book. That is what I dislike about the modern world - there is a great necessity for precision, uniformity, analysis - so that dreams, music, even emotions, all the most beautiful things in life must be explained into dull science and lose all the mystery which makes them charming. However, despite my profound aversion to modern life, I sensed that I would be able to form a bond with you, which is why I allowed the vampire boy to take a copy of the book. You have been receiving messages in the form of dreams from the ghost Margaret, is that not so?'

'Yes, although not for about a fortnight,' explained Ada. 'When I was having the dreams, there were moments which were as clear as day, but most of the time they were shrouded in a veil of obscurity, so that I could only catch glimpses of things. It was as if something was blocking the messages, so that only little details filtered through. I still feel she is trying to communicate with me, but for some reason the barrier is now impenetrable.'

'I see,' pondered Geoffrey. 'Have you had any other experiences of dreams before this?'

'No,' she replied. 'Ever since I can remember, I've always had very vivid and unusual dreams, but this is the first time I have experienced any which signified anything. This is quite strange, as I've been in the school for a couple of years now, but this is the first encounter I've had with Margret, even though she has been a ghost for five years.'

'It often happens that the ability to receive and interpret messages in dreams does not develop until a certain age,' he explained. 'In fact, you are unusually young to have already discovered it, and something tells me that you have a great talent, which should be nurtured. At any rate, the messages transmitted by ghosts are often incomplete and erratic, for they do not have the true gift of imparting dreams, only a limited ability resembling it which is only acquired after death. The best way is to enter the ghost's subconscious and see for yourself what she herself may not consciously know, and this will lead you to unravelling the mystery of her death. Of course, ghosts do not sleep, but they still dream - they often go into a trance in which they relive their death.'

'Do you think I could enter her mind?' asked Ada excitedly. 'How would I do that?'

'There is no such thing as a method for our art,' Geoffrey replied. 'It is not possible to teach it in the usual way, rather you must discover it for yourself. But you must be careful - when you enter the mind of another, you effectively merge your spirit temporarily with theirs. Unless you have someone in the outside world to watch over you and bring you back within yourself, it is possible to become lost in the mind of the other person. As a result, you will seem to be in a coma from which only very powerful magic can wake you, and the person whose mind you have entered will succumb to insanity. However, do not be alarmed: when the time comes, you will know instinctively what to do.'

'I see, but how will the other person with me know when and how to pull me out of Margaret's mind?'

Geoffrey chuckled, 'You ask a great many questions, Ada, as if this were something scientific. If I were you, I would ask Rupert to be your guardian, that is, your companion on the journey who still remains firmly in the real world. I know you might feel more comfortable with your friend Beatrice, since she is a girl, but it is necessary for your guardian to have supernatural abilities as well. The vampire boy will do very nicely indeed, being both very talented in magic and very much attached to you.' As she was about to interrupt, he added authoritatively, 'I happen to know he dreams about you. Now, you must have some object in which you will pour a little of your soul. He must keep it, which will enable him to follow you into Margaret's mind, while maintaining his own consciousness. If he feels you are in danger or have been immersed for too long, he will use this object to call you back.'

'What object is this, though, and where will I get it?' asked Ada.

'That I do not yet know. You will find it within the book. The scenery around you is not real: I have created it in your mind, just like in a dream. You must explore the book with your thoughts, the scene will change as you desire, and then you will find your talisman. When day comes, I must vanish, but you will still have it, and then you can give it to Rupert in the morning.'

When he had finished speaking, Ada walked to the edge of the cliff, a little uncertain about his very vague instruction. She closed her eyes and imagined the sun setting over beautiful mountains. A strange, tingling sensation ran through her veins. A moment later, she opened her eyes again, and was pleasantly surprised. The previous scene had vanished: she was standing in an Alpine valley carpeted with vibrant flowers. Birds twittered and chirped merrily and in the distance, the sound of cows nonchalantly mooing wafted along the breeze. The sky behind the majestic peaks was a clear blue, but the dying rays of the sun stained the clouds pink and gold, like a rose garden in the sky.

Slowly and silently, a fragment of one of the clouds began to fall gently down to earth. As it came to rest in front of her eyes, it transformed into a glistening ruby set in a delicate gold ring. The stone was so clear that it seemed to contain unfathomable depths, like a crimson lake. Wonderingly, Ada took the ring and slipped it onto her finger. It fitted perfectly.

'Good heavens!' cried Geoffrey's voice, very close to her all of sudden. 'Is it really...? Yes, it is definitely her ring.'

'Whose ring is it?' asked Ada, intrigued.

'It is an old heirloom of my family,' he explained. 'It was passed down for centuries from mother to daughter, on my mother's side of the family. As I was the only child, it came to me, and I made it my talisman. When I got married, I gave it to my wife. Her name was Adeline, she was the most beautiful woman in all the world and I adored her. She was not one of the Dream Givers, but she had been my dearest friend from childhood, and later she became both my guardian and my wife. Alas, she died while still in the fullest blossom of her beauty, and she had no child,' a break came into his voice, as though he were on the brink of tears, 'but as she lay on her deathbed, she gave me back the ring and a prophecy. Her prophecies always used to come true. She asked me to bury the ring within the Book of Dreams where nobody but I could find it and said that after many centuries, a girl would awaken me from the pages. She said that the girl who found my ring would be our spiritual heir and would carry on my gift; I was warned that she would come to me in the most unlikely of places, and as always, she was right. Though I had no direct descendants, you, Ada, are the child of my soul.'

Before she could say anything in reply, the scene began to fade into a thick mist. There was a great rush of wind and a roaring like the ocean.

'What's happening?' she asked, alarmed.

'My time is short: morning is almost here, and ghosts and dreams must retreat into the remnants of the night,' Geoffrey's voice sounded so far away.

'Wait, come back! I have so much to ask you.'//
'I wish I could. You must return to see me soon.'//
'Before you go, let me see your face,' she pleaded.//
'One day, but not now,' he sighed and vanished, leaving her all alone in the bleak light of day.

CHAPTER 10 - IN THE ARCHIVE

When Geoffrey had left her, the pages of the book were stiff and silent, just like any ordinary book. All of a sudden, she felt so lonely without him. He had started to show her who she really was. Though she had not slept all night, she was just as refreshed and alert as if she had just woken from long slumber. The ring was still on her finger, and the crimson ruby seemed to draw her into its depths. Excitedly, she thought of all Geoffrey had told her, and all which she had yet to learn. As she waited for it to be time to get up, she was already happily anticipating her next trip into the Book of Dreams.

At breakfast she announced to her friends that she had penetrated the mystery of the book.

'Oh, wonderful!' cried Rupert, impressed. 'What have you found out?'

'Calm down and don't talk so loudly,' Ada admonished him, though her eyes were sparkling with just as much excitement as his. 'Apparently, it is possible to enter Margaret's subconscious to find out what really happened. We just need to find her and get her to join in with the plan.'

'How do you do that?' asked Beatrice.

'I don't actually know,' replied Ada. 'According to Geoffrey, it's not something that can be taught, and there is in fact no method, but he thinks I will know instinctively what to do when the time comes.'

'Who is Geoffrey?' asked Rupert dubiously.

'A voice inside the book. He is the author,' she explained. 'Rupert, it was the most wonderful experience. He is so lovely and wise and I am sure he will be able to guide us.'

'What does he look like?' interjected Bertie.

'Well, I don't know. He is just a disembodied voice, but he said that one day he would show me his face. Anyway, I don't think that's very relevant.'

'No, it isn't really,' agreed Rupert. 'However, this Geoffrey appears to think he is establishing a long-term relationship with you,' he observed gravely.

'Yes, of course he is,' replied Ada, surprised that he could think anything different. 'He said I was his spiritual heir, the child of his soul. You see, within the world of the Book of Dreams, there was a beautiful mountain valley, and a magical ring fell from the sky, which fulfilled a prophecy. Rupert, you seem disapproving.'

'I'm not,' he said hastily. 'It's just that I haven't met this Geoffrey, so I want to make quite sure that he is not practising dark magic. Can I see the ring, please?'

'Certainly, and there's no need at all to be suspicious about Geoffrey. If you heard his voice, you would be convinced, for it has a gentle, melodious quality which inspires perfect trust,' she placed the ring on the table, and they all looked at it in awe.

Rupert picked it up and studied it carefully, then announced, 'It looks fine to me. What are you meant to do with it?'

'Geoffrey said that I might get too deeply immersed in Margaret's mind, so you need to use the ring to call me back. However, he did not specify how.'

'You mean that I am to be your guardian,' he said. 'I have heard stories about this before, and I think the talisman does most of the work by itself, so I'm sure I'll manage.'

'When are you going to do it?' asked Bertie.

'Whenever we can find Margaret,' replied Ada. 'Until then, I thought we could explore the archive.'

'Won't people think it a bit strange?' asked Beatrice.

'I'm sure we can think of a good reason without compromising the investigation,' said Ada. 'At any rate, if this rain carries on, we will be indoors at break, so nobody will notice.'

'That's a good point,' she replied. 'By the way, I've just had a thought: it's just possible that Margaret could be there, in the archive, now that the caretaker has banned ghosts in the music building. You see, she would be undisturbed, as I'm quite sure that nobody goes in there very often at all.'

'Indeed,' Rupert got up, 'we are making progress! I suggest we meet up at the archive at the start of morning break.'

This proposition was enthusiastically agreed to,

and the four friends went to lessons full of lively anticipation. As Ada predicted, the rain continued with no sign of abatement, a dismal grey sky glaring down upon the school. As soon as the bell rang shrilly for break, they slipped through the library and shut themselves into the archive. Rows upon rows of shelves, crammed with weary, dusty books, towered above them. The floor was scattered with files which had fallen down, and Bertie tripped over a pile of them, releasing a great cloud of dust. Wedged onto a table in the corner of the archive, which was hardly more than a closet, was an ancient and rather battered computer.

Rupert glanced at it dismissively, 'I don't think I'll bother with that; we'll start on the files, shall we?'

He perched on the edge of the table and picked one up at random. His green eyes flashed like lightning: the pages flicked themselves quickly, hundreds of words rushing before him in a few seconds.

'Nothing,' he pronounced. 'How many of these are there?'

'This might be more useful - it's from 2014, the year Margaret died,' said Ada.

'Ah, thank you,' Rupert flew through the pages, then pointed excitedly, 'look at this! I'm sure it's her... yes, and there's Isolda. She looks a little familiar, though I couldn't say why.'

What had attracted his attention was a photograph in an old newsletter from the year of Margaret's death. They gathered around Rupert and pored over the photo, which had been taken at the House Challenge competition. Margaret and Isolda stood in the middle, with radiant but slightly exaggerated smiles, holding either handle of the trophy. On Margaret's left, an awkward, eleven-year-old Ernest peered out of the page; on Isolda's right, a boy they did not recognise. Underneath the picture was the rather uninteresting caption: Margaret, Isolda, Ernest, Archie - winners of the 2014 House Challenge.'

'Well, I don't see what that tells you,' complained Bertie. 'However, I also feel as if I had seen Isolda before. As Rupert says, she appears familiar, though I think it's mostly her eyes.'

They tried to remember where they had seen her before, but with no success. Isolda's blue eyes stared back at them, revealing nothing. Rupert shrugged and continued to flick through the pages of the file.

'Ah, this should be more informative,' he observed presently. 'This newsletter is from a few months later. "Congratulations to the sixth formers who have been awarded places at Oxford and Cambridge,"' he read aloud. '"Isolda G and Margaret H have been accepted by Urganda College, Oxford, to study biology and classics, respectively."'

'That's the college Miss Gourlay went to,' Ada pointed out. 'It's quite likely she would have known Isolda, especially as she studied biology and they would be about the same age.'

Before anyone could reply, she felt a damp, cold touch on her shoulder. Startled, she turned around. Margaret hovered behind her, translucent and glowing eerily in the garish lights of the archive.

'Hello, Ada,' she smiled. 'I have missed you.'

'I have too,' replied Ada. 'We looked for you everywhere, but we couldn't find you.'

'It is no longer safe for me to haunt the music department,' Margaret explained, 'so I remain here where nobody will disturb me.'

Rupert asked curiously, 'Why must you remain in hiding? Is there someone trying to prevent you from communicating with us?'

Margaret was about to reply, when suddenly a look of terror seized her. Her silvery form started to fade. Rupert sprang to his feet and grasped her hands just before they could vanish into air.

'Margaret, stay!' he cried. 'Don't be afraid,' he added gently. 'We want to help you, but you have to confide in us. What happened just now?'

'He was here,' she whispered tremulously. 'Not in person, but I could feel his power. He will never let me be free.'

'Who is he?' asked Rupert. 'And how do you know it's a man?'

'I don't know, I just feel it is a man. Whoever he is, he is using powerful magic, and that is why I am afraid. He is close to us, I can feel the power of his presence. He is in the school itself and he is always watching us,' she glanced around furtively, then continued, 'Every day, I have been trying to enter your dreams again, Ada, but he has always prevented me, so that I felt faint and sick every time I tried to reach out to you. Rupert, you are a vampire, you must know about magic: how is he doing this?'

Rupert frowned, 'I would have to investigate further, but this I know for sure: it is powerful magic indeed which can command the dead. Anyhow, we only have ten minutes, and we have a plan, but I'm not sure if it will work.'

Ada explained quickly about the Book of Dreams, and Margaret eagerly agreed to try it. Until this moment, Ada had been very unsure about what to do, but all of a sudden, the path ahead was illuminated by a bright ray of light. She closed her eyes and held Margaret's hands. They were like clear water to touch. The others watched anxiously as they both seemed to go into a trance. Rupert fiddled with the ring she had given him, excited but apprehensive.

A moment later, Ada felt the whole world becoming dark, as she entered the shady depths of Margaret's memories. Then the thick night cleared as suddenly as it had fallen. She found herself in one of the large rooms on the top floor of St Anthony's house, where the sixth formers slept. The rose red dawn was creeping through a chink in the curtains. Silently, Isolda was getting dressed and, looking around her furtively, crept out of the room.

As Ada hurried after her, she caught sight of herself in the mirror and realised that she had become Margaret. Isolda made straight for the castle ruins. Ada followed at a distance, thoroughly perplexed. They both climbed the precarious spiral staircase up to the remains of the tower.

Isolda took a deep breath and steadied her trembling hands. Obviously thinking she was alone, she began to chant to herself in a low voice, strange incantations which Ada could not understand. Becoming more and more animated, she waved her arms and threw back her head, a cascade of golden hair tumbling over her shoulders. A gale began to howl, and she seemed to direct the winds with her mysterious chant.

Suddenly, the earth below seemed to shudder and a gaping chasm formed. Isolda turned around, apprehensive for a moment. When she saw that she was not alone, confusion and horror snatched the colour from her face.

'Margaret,' she stammered.

Immediately, darkness engulfed everything. Ada felt like she was falling down into the depths of the earth. There were shadows above her, shadows which moved and talked animatedly, but she could not comprehend what they were saying. Panicking, she called out to Rupert. The darkness swallowed up her feeble voice.

'Ada, are you alright?' Rupert anxiously slipped the magic ring onto her finger.

She opened her eyes and found herself back in the archive. 'Yes,' she faltered.

Suddenly, she crumpled and fell into Rupert's arms. A ghostly pallor suffused her cheeks. She was as cold as ice. Though wide open, her eyes were vacant and glassy.

The cold hands of despair grasped Rupert's heart. He looked to Margaret for reassurance, but she was already fading away.

'Rupert, look after her. I can't stay any longer,' her voice sounded stifled.

The next instant, she was gone. Then it dawned on Rupert that Ada had not fainted. She had been enchanted. Though his heart was fluttering wildly against his chest, he forced himself to be calm.

'I'll go and get a teacher,' suggested Beatrice.

'No! That is what you absolutely must not do,' cried Rupert. 'This is magic, she's not ill at all. Human interference could make it worse.'

'What should we do?' asked Bertie.

'Stay here; leave everything to me. Nobody must find out about this.'

'We only have five minutes,' pointed out Beatrice.

'I hope it's enough,' replied Rupert.

He drew a doorway in the air, and a long tunnel materialised at once. When he had stepped through the portal, the air remained glowing faintly for a few seconds. Rupert felt the wind rushing in his ears, then found himself at home, in the laboratory.

For a moment, he was slightly baffled by the vast array of bottles and dried herbs. However, an inspiration seized him, and he was no longer the slightest bit indecisive. He nodded at a selection of the bottles. Obediently, they floated over and poured their contents into a beaker. The petals of a flower which only bloomed in the full moon followed. Eyes flashing, he blew gently on the mixture, muttering something he did not quite understand himself. It was as if the urgency of the situation had made all his ignorance melt away and magic flow from his fingertips without conscious thought, like some half-forgotten memory. The petals dissolved into the liquid, and the beaker glowed softly. Rupert grabbed a small, emerald green bottle and nodded at the beaker. It obligingly transferred the correct amount to the bottle.

A few seconds later, he appeared out of thin air in the archive. Beatrice and Bertie breathed a sigh of relief. Though it felt like an eternity, he had only been gone three minutes. Tenderly, Rupert moistened Ada's lips with a few drops of the potion.

'What is it?' asked Bertie.

'A cure for all ills,' replied Rupert. 'That is, all magic-induced ills.'

They waited tensely. The ticking of Bertie's watch was deafening.

After a moment, Ada opened her eyes and sat up. 'What just happened?' she asked, bemused.

'I don't know exactly, but it was definitely caused by magic. Are you alright?'

'Yes, absolutely. Thank you, Rupert,' she stood up, a little unsteadily. 'Well, maybe not completely yet.'

'I don't think you should try that again,' remarked Rupert gravely. 'It appears very dangerous.'

'But I found out so much,' she protested. 'I think I'd only need one more trip to uncover the whole story.'

'I'm still dubious about Geoffrey and the Book of Dreams,' Rupert frowned. 'I don't want to put you in danger.'

'Oh Rupert, you are becoming such a fussy boy when it comes to magic,' she chuckled. 'It's very sweet of you to be concerned about me in this way, but I can take care of myself, you know. And whatever happened, I'm sure it wasn't Geoffrey's fault.'

'Well, if you say so, but...' began Rupert.

'Yes, but you still think you would take care of me better than I would of myself, is that it?' she laughed at his serious, blushing face. 'You may be a vampire, but you are still living in the twenty-first century, where your clumsy though well-intentioned attempts at chivalry are a little out of date and may offend many ardent feminists. However, rest assured that I will inform you before I do anything radical, even if I don't listen to your advice.'

Before Rupert could puzzle out her remark about his outdated attempts at chivalry - he had always been under the impression that he was a model of the modern gentleman - the bell shrilly summoned them to lessons.

In the interim till lunch time, the friends had no opportunity to discuss the morning's events. However, Rupert had much leisure to brood on them, since the geography lesson did not occupy too much of his concentration. He was troubled by what Margaret had told them and wondered who the mysterious man could be, of whom she appeared so terrified. Despite Ada's great confidence in the Book of Dreams, he became gradually more distrustful of it and began to wish he had not introduced her to it in the first place.

As soon as they sat down to lunch, Rupert asked Ada, 'What did you see when you entered Margaret's mind?'

She reported to them everything that had happened, concluding, 'Isolda was a witch, and Margaret accidentally found out. I don't know what exactly Isolda was trying to do, but she seemed horrified at being discovered. Before I could see any more, everything went dark, but I think this is circumstantial evidence that Isolda could have killed Margaret, the motive being to conceal whatever Margaret had witnessed.'

Rupert agreed, 'It certainly looks like that. Now at least we have a suspect, which should make the investigation easier.'

'What do you propose to do next?' asked Beatrice.

'I think we should try to find out more about Isolda and see if we can discover more evidence,' replied Ada. 'And although I do understand there is a risk, Rupert, I think we need to penetrate Margaret's memories again to discover the exact circumstances of her death.'

'Perhaps Isolda was looking for the miniature of the witch in the legend,' suggested Bertie. 'It is said to be still in the castle grounds.'

'Yes, it's possible. I will try to find out more about this miniature,' said Rupert. 'Also, since she was a witch and went to Urganda College, I imagine she would probably be in the Oxford League of Witches.'

'Do you think it would be possible to trace her?' asked Ada.

Rupert pensively nibbled his garlic bread and remarked, 'It would be difficult. Being a witch, she would easily be able to change her identity using potions. However, the League would always know where she is. The only problem is, I can't really just ask them for the information; they are extremely secretive.'

'Rupert,' interrupted Bertie, 'are you sure you can eat garlic bread?'

'Yes, I've taken my tablets,' he explained. 'At any rate, to return to the point, there is one thing I want to find out: who is so desperate to conceal the circumstances of Margaret's death that they torment her ghost and enchant Ada to stop her finding out?'

'Isolda herself, perhaps,' suggested Beatrice.

'My instinct tells me it isn't,' said Rupert, 'mainly because Margaret mentioned a man. I think we can safely assume that this man also made Ada faint. Also, this man is relatively close to us, maybe even in the school, or he would not be able to act so quickly and effectively - any magic which involves controlling the mind requires relatively close proximity to work.'

'But who is the man?' asked Beatrice. 'Was he her accomplice?'

'I really couldn't say,' replied Rupert. 'We must not rule out any possibilities. By the way, Ada, may I borrow the Book of Dreams?'

'If you like, although I don't see what purpose it would serve,' she replied.

'Merely a caprice of mine,' he assured her. 'I just want to completely reassure myself about it.'

Wondering at his unusually closed-minded attitude, she nevertheless readily agreed to his request. That night, he lay awake for a long time, perusing the book in the darkness under the covers, but making nothing of it. He had just decided that perhaps the best thing to do would be to take it back to the Universal Vampire Library and bury it in oblivion, when the book seemed to sense his thoughts. All of a sudden, the pages illuminated and sucked him into the parchment.

When he emerged, he found himself on a barren mountain, gazing down at a treacherous ravine below. The wind nipped sharply at his cheeks. A raven swooped across the glowering sky, hoarsely croaking prophecies of doom.

From the chasm, a thunderous voice grumbled, 'Why do you bother me with your ridiculous suspicions? Not only have you questioned my integrity, but you now want to put me back in the library and break the connection I have formed with Ada. I am deeply offended!'

'Well,' said Rupert, rather taken aback, 'I only wanted you to help with the investigation, not to suggest highly dangerous activities to Ada, so I really think it is time to break off the damaging connection.'

'What happened is hardly my fault. In fact, I think Ada's first trip was a great success,' remarked Geoffrey, this time from the sky.

'She could have gone into a coma, and you call that a great success!' retorted Rupert. 'Anyhow, I think you might have taught her a little better rather than letting her do everything by trial and error.'

'Do not talk about things you do not understand, child,' he admonished condescendingly, so close to Rupert that he jumped.

'I may not know anything about this particular branch of magic, but even I can tell that you have been extraordinarily negligent about health and safety. Either you don't know what you're doing yourself, or you don't care about her, or perhaps you intended for this to happen all along. Which is it?' demanded Rupert angrily.

'I am really astonished that Ada associates with you so closely, for you are a very ill-mannered and irritating boy, not at all suitable company for such a nice, refined girl. You have insulted me,' with this remark, a fork of lightening flashed through the sky and thunder rumbled all around the mountain.

'Well, why don't you demand satisfaction then?' cried Rupert recklessly, eyes flashing.

'I am not in the habit of duelling, not being a vampire - they are for some reason extraordinarily addicted to this somewhat vulgar occupation - but I cannot decline what is tantamount to a challenge,' replied Geoffrey sombrely. 'I suppose I had better make myself visible.'

'Yes please, I find disembodied voices slightly disconcerting, especially as Mr Mond says they are a clear indication of psychological issues.'

'Very well, but you must not be frivolous,' suddenly, he appeared before Rupert in a cloud of smoke.

'Indeed, I am being quite serious,' replied Rupert airily, although he was a little put out by the almost giant proportions and formidable aspect of the author of the Book of Dreams.

Nevertheless, he was determined not to back down, despite feeling he had been a little foolish, and had fortunately read enough French novels to put on a reasonably good imitation of the manners of duellists. Indeed, it would have almost been perfect, if only he were not dressed in a nightshirt. The air grew cold and it began to rain dismally.

'The weather isn't very nice in this book,' he observed, 'I'm surprised Ada enjoyed it so much.'

'Oh, I made it sunny for her,' explained Geoffrey. 'Come on, here's a sword.' Rupert tried not to look surprised at a sword falling out of the sky. 'En garde!'

Rupert's heart fluttered with nervous excitement as they circled each other. The ground was slippery from the rain, which continued to drive into his face savagely. Occasionally, he made a thrust as fast as lightning, but mostly found himself parrying rapidly. At the same time, he felt the whole affair was very ridiculous and wished he had not been so provocative.

'You've never fought a duel before, have you?' asked Geoffrey after a few minutes.

'No, but there's a first time for everything,' he replied coolly.

'Indeed. I'm surprised you're managing so well with such erratic technique.'

'The technique is a combination of elementary fencing lessons and practical application of descriptions in Dumas novels.'

Throwing caution to the winds, he sprang forwards and managed to force his opponent to the edge of the precipice. Their swords clanged together. Suddenly, Rupert saw a flash of steel close to his eyes. Instinctively, he threw his hands up in front of his face and muttered an incantation under his breath. Flames appeared and danced between his fingers. Tongues of fire licked Geoffrey's sword, which became so hot that he dropped it at once.

'I think that we had better leave it at that before either of us gets mortally wounded,' remarked Rupert, blowing out the flames.

'I completely agree, and I also think we had better not tell Ada about this - um... incident,' replied Geoffrey. 'I hope I can rely on your discretion.'

'Of course. She would probably reprimand me if she found out, for she's quite fond of you, but I'll be able to inform her in the morning that I'm now going to be sensible and listen to her in the future. Having said that,' he continued somewhat haughtily, 'she can't expect me to share her innocent confidence in everyone she meets, particularly magical beings who get her into dangerous situations, and I'm sure she would appreciate my good intentions.'

Geoffrey chuckled, 'Yes, I did notice that in her artless way she spoke of me so favourably that you got quite jealous.'

'I suppose I did,' admitted Rupert, 'but I was also dubious because you wouldn't show her your face.'

'Would you like to see my face, then, to reassure you completely?' he asked.

'Well, I can see you right now.'

'Ah, but you forget that you are in a waking dream, where nothing is what it seems.'

As he spoke, the rain gave way to gentle sunshine and Geoffrey himself transformed from a fierce giant into a little gnome-like man with laughing, twinkling eyes.

'I have reflected, and come to the conclusion that you are perhaps right about health and safety - a dreadfully modern concept, but if even the vampires have moved on, I too must keep up with the times. I am not quite sure how, though.'

'I'm sure you could consult Mr Mond about it,' laughed Rupert.

'You are again being frivolous,' admonished Geoffrey. 'What I meant is this: it is quite normal to experience faintness or nausea after attempting something as difficult as what Ada did, but the feeling soon passes, and it is only through aspiring to greater heights than what can be quite safely achieved that her powers will grow. However, what occurred in the archive was actually quite dangerous and certainly not a consequence of mere mental exhaustion. Rupert, it has become clear to me that witchcraft is at work here - it bears all the hallmarks of dark magic of the sort practised these days by the Oxford League of Witches, and I am therefore unable to advise Ada on the subject.'

'So you think there is a witch in the school?'

'Yes, they must be here at St Jude's, but more I cannot tell. You must be very careful. What will you do next?'

'I'm not sure, I will have to discuss with Ada, but everything seems to be leading to the League.'

At that moment, they were startled by the shrill ringing of a bell.

'The school bell,' remarked Geoffrey. 'I'd better release you from the book.'

There was a rush of wind in his ears, and a light at the end of a long tunnel. The light grew brighter and brighter until Rupert found himself lying in bed, a little breathless, and blinking in the cold light of morning. Bertie called to him to hurry up and dress, which he promptly did, while filling his friend in on the most recent developments in a whisper.

'Good heavens!' Bertie whispered back. 'I must say that vampires are very uncivilised if they still go in for duelling.'

'Well, so were humans until relatively recent history,' Rupert pointed out.

'I suppose,' Bertie conceded. 'Anyhow, Rosaline thought you were a very eligible future boyfriend for Ada, as long as you always listen to her rather than doing silly things on impulse.'

'What? When?' demanded Rupert.

'When we went to your house and you were in the library. I think it was meant to be a confidential discussion among girls, but I thought I'd tell you.'

'Oh, well,' Rupert blushed, 'let's go downstairs. I need to give the book back to Ada, and I'm thinking that on the weekend I can try and find out about the League of Witches, so we need to consult the girls about the investigation. And Bertie, not a word about last night please.'

'Of course not, old chap,' laughed Bertie, and they clattered down the stairs to breakfast.

'Although,' added Rupert, 'despite the duel perhaps being what Rosaline would call a silly thing on impulse, I am very pleased to have sorted out the matter of the Book of Dreams.'

At this point, the girls also came down to breakfast and Ada said, 'Hello Rupert, was your perusal of the book satisfactory?'

'Extremely,' he replied, passing it to her under the table. 'I spoke to Geoffrey and he has taken my advice about health and safety. He also said that a member of the Oxford League of Witches is in the school and we must be very careful. I shall clearly have to investigate the League.'

Having delivered this slightly ominous news and been thanked by Ada for his efforts, he turned his attention to a croissant.

CHAPTER 11 - THE LEAGUE OF WITCHES

When the weekend came, Ada was quite exhausted by the developments of the last few days, particularly those concerning her newly discovered magic. She felt rather lost without any guidance, apart from the somewhat disorganised kind provided by Geoffrey, so she determined to consult her parents. The right time arose on the Saturday afternoon, when the three of them were enjoying the mellow autumn sunshine in the garden and her parents had momentarily stopped discussing work and other tedious matters.

'Mummy, Daddy, I have something serious to discuss with you.'

'Oh dear. I hope it's not a boyfriend, darling,' replied her father teasingly.

'Certainly not.'

'How is Rupert, by the way? That is the name of your friend, isn't it?' he pursued. 'You haven't mentioned him lately.'

'Rupert is fine; I have also discovered that he is a

vampire, which brings me on to the point.'

'What?' interrupted her father. 'Well, well!'

'I'm not actually that surprised, Ada,' remarked her mother. 'I suspected when you mentioned about the tablets which could not be identified, as well as the strange tendency of knowing something before it happens and the occasional desire to consume vast amounts of black pudding. But do carry on.'

Slightly surprised, Ada told them everything about the ghost, about how Rupert had given her the Book of Dreams and what had ensued. Her parents listened to the account gravely, though not expressing any astonishment, as she had expected.

When she had finished, her mother smiled, 'Ada, I am very happy that you have inherited the gift of the Dream Givers. My grandmother possessed it too, but as it did not appear in the generations after - neither my mother nor I have had it in the slightest degree - I assumed it was lost in our family. Therefore, it never occurred to me to tell you about it.'

'Oh, Mummy, I am relieved. When it first started happening, I thought I might be going mad.'

'Well, perhaps Mr Mond had better not know about it, or he might be concerned,' she laughed.

'Indeed. You were a lot more open-minded than I expected actually, especially about my having a vampire for a close friend.'

'Well, the vampires are very well integrated, though they have their eccentricities. Besides, I am in general very open-minded, don't you think, dear?' she turned to her husband.

'Oh yes, very open-minded. Dr Botherby was very surprised, I remember, that with such a clever daughter you were not a formidable and pushy mother,' he laughed.

Meanwhile, Rupert was busy setting about his investigations. He shut himself in his room and ran his fingers over the mirror, singing quietly to himself in a hypnotic tone, 'Rosaline, Rosaline.' Presently, the mirror clouded over and Rosaline's face appeared out of the swirling mist.

'Hello Rupert,' she smiled. 'I presume you have some exciting news, since it could not wait to be told by letter.'

'Yes, so much has happened this week. Ada managed to penetrate the mystery of the Book of Dreams and enter Margaret's subconscious. We have discovered that her friend Isolda was a witch, and Margaret accidentally stumbled upon her performing some kind of spell. She is our main suspect at the moment, as it seems that she and Margaret were alone on the day of her death. However, Margaret told us about a mysterious man who is trying to prevent her from making appearances, and so it appears that there is a member of the League of Witches in our midst. I just don't know what the connection is between this man and Isolda.'

'Well, you have certainly discovered a great deal; it's all very exciting,' Rosaline's eyes sparkled like stars. 'Do you happen to know what Isolda was trying to achieve with her incantations?'

'No, but this happened at the castle ruins outside

the school. There is a legend surrounding this castle which my friend Ernest told me about: apparently, a witch named Isolda once married the lord of the castle and on her deathbed, she locked her soul in a miniature portrait of her which would perpetuate her curse on all his dynasty. Of course, humans are often wrong about these things, but do you think there is anything in this legend?'

'Yes there is ,' she informed him. 'The witch Isolda was the most powerful sorceress that England had ever known - some say she was descended from Hecate herself - but she used her power for great evil among the witch community. Eventually, all the other witches united to help her husband imprison her. The miniature you refer to is a very powerful relic: whoever can unlock the soul of Isolda from it would be able to conquer the world, but at a terrible price. From that moment, they will have no will but that of Isolda, no purpose but hers, which is the subjugation of the other magical races and the destruction of humans. Fortunately, this dangerous relic was believed to be lost, but it appears that it has been found again.'

'Do you think the League is behind this?' he asked.

'Undoubtedly. It is highly unlikely that a girl of seventeen could attempt to unlock the relic without help from witches much more powerful than her,' said Rosaline. 'Clearly, she failed, but now that the League knows where it is, they will persist with the quest.'

'I see. That must be the political trouble among the witches which I have heard mentioned, but wasn't really listening to, for I can't imagine the entire community wants to release this evil spirit.'

'Indeed, they do not. The majority of the League itself would rather the portrait remained lost forever, but a small, extremist group within the League is determined to find it and use it to gain domination of all Britain.'

'Rosaline, I am going to get into the League and see for myself exactly what this extremist group are planning,' announced Rupert.

She looked slightly shocked, 'Rupert, they are dangerous. If you get caught, not only would you be in great personal danger, but it could precipitate a diplomatic catastrophe.'

'Aren't you being a little dramatic?' he laughed.

'Not at all. Of course we spy on the witches and they spy on us, but diplomacy is maintained because all the spying is done in an unobtrusive way. Anyhow, what do you intend to do exactly?'

'I need your advice on that,' he replied thoughtfully. 'They must have meetings at Oxford. Perhaps I could sneak into one and eavesdrop. Or I could go in when they're not there and look at the minutes. Although I suppose they might not contain the information I want because the extremist sector may not want to reveal their plans to the rest. You know, I think the best time to eavesdrop would not be at a meeting but at some kind of social gathering, where there would be enough people to provide cover.'

'Rupert,' interrupted Rosaline with a smile, 'you have asked my advice and then given a long monologue without waiting for the answer, but I take pleasure from advising, so this is my opinion: your last idea is the best. It so happens that tonight is a full moon and the witches will be celebrating the festival of Hecate, which always happens on the full moon of October. There will certainly be a party at Oxford, which all members of the League would attend, and to which many would bring their spouses and children even if they are not members, so you will be able to hide in the crowd.'

'That's brilliant!' he cried. 'I will be there. The only slight problem is how to get from Wales to Oxford without my parents noticing.'

'I would think that the Bodleian Library must be connected to the Vampire Library. If you can find the portal, you will be able to travel instantly to Oxford,' she glanced behind her into the room which Rupert could not see. 'I must go now, but I expect you to write to me so that I can enjoy the adventure second hand.'

'Of course I will. Thank you for all the information.'

'You're welcome; this is where a traditional vampire education is useful! Be careful, and good luck.'

'Don't worry about me, Rosaline: I'm always lucky and in any case, this time I have meticulously planned the campaign ahead,' he smiled and waved goodbye as she disappeared into the mirror.

After Rosaline had gone, Rupert remained sitting on his bed in an attitude of profound contemplation. It would of course be necessary to disguise himself in order to avoid being caught, and he would have to be as unobtrusive as possible. Suddenly, an inspiration seized him. Jumping up, he clattered down the many flights of stairs to the kitchen, where Hawkins the butler sat majestically reading a newspaper and directing the preparation of a roast duck with his eyes.

'Hello, Hawkins,' said Rupert. 'Are you busy?'

'Never too busy to converse with you,' replied Hawkins affably, while sternly waving the salt and pepper grinders back to their places. 'Would you like to try one of my petits milles feuilles, milord?'

'Thanks very much,' Rupert sat down and diligently ate a pastry. 'Hawkins, I require your help for an enterprise of the utmost importance, and I must also impose upon you the greatest secrecy before I reveal my plans to you.'

'That, milord, is not a very reassuring start, but you may confide in me,' replied Hawkins.

'Good. I am planning to secretly enter the Oxford League of Witches. They are holding a party tonight in honour of the festival of Hecate.'

Hawkins raised one eyebrow very slightly, signifying his horror at the proposal, 'I would very strongly advise against it. Ah, but I can see from your expression that I am wasting my breath. May I enquire what the purpose of this escapade is?'

'You certainly may, Hawkins, but I haven't got time to enlighten you right now,' said Rupert. 'I need you to help me remain incognito: I have decided to appear as a waiter, so can you please advise me on how to look like a waiter?'

'Well, it is a delicate art which cannot be rushed,' began Hawkins, 'but I will try to explain to you the most important principles. You must always be very elegant and not run around the table like a headless chicken, so make sure you serve the dishes to the guests in order of where they are sitting. When pouring wine, do not be miserly, but also avoid filling the glass completely. Where a sauce is to be poured onto something once it is on the table, this should be done in a synchronised manner. Therefore, pour the sauce yourself for two people and make the sauce boats do it themselves at the same time for the rest.'

'But Hawkins,' interrupted Rupert, 'how do human waiters manage?'

'They are not as good at it as we vampires,' he observed haughtily. 'Anyway, when serving potatoes…'

'Yes, thank you, I don't need the complete guide, just the basics,' said Rupert hastily. 'We might be here all evening otherwise. Now, could I borrow some of your clothes, please?'

'If you are going to be among witches, you will require black robes,' he replied. 'Let me see, I think I have some in the cupboard, from when I infiltrated a similar gathering, when your parents were still working for intelligence. Ah, here you are. Put it on.'

Dubiously, Rupert put on the voluminous black robes, which were rather too wide for him and trailed on the floor, 'I look like I'm wearing a dress, they fit so badly!' he complained.

'Hmm… they need taking in a bit,' observed Hawkins, 'but I think you'd better just grow rather than shortening them. Otherwise you will still look like a child.'

Rupert closed his eyes and ran his fingers up and down the folds in the fabric. The robes immediately fitted him. He snapped his fingers and a bottle of purple liquid floated over from the laboratory. Carefully, he poured a few drops into a glass.

'Don't make yourself look too old,' advised Hawkins. 'It is traditional at this festival for new members to wait at table, so that no outsiders are there. I also suggest you conceal your fangs.'

Rupert nodded and drank the glass all in one go. The taste was unusual, though not unpleasant. For a few moments, nothing happened. Then a strange warmth began to diffuse slowly through his whole body, as if he were glowing inside, and he realised he was growing on the spot. When the potion had done its work, about five years seemed to have crept upon him in an instant, and, he thought with satisfaction, he resembled in all points a harmless and unobtrusive undergraduate.

'What do you think?' he asked, and his voice sounded lower than usual.

'Excellent, milord,' Hawkins' mouth twitched into what was almost a smile. 'You had better take a dagger, just in case. Good luck, and don't forget about the principles of being a good waiter.'

'Thank you, I will remember,' Rupert drew a dagger out of the air, concealed it beneath the many folds of his costume and left Hawkins tutting to himself over the roast duck.

He opened the secret panel in the library and slipped into the entrance hall of the Vampire Library.

This time, he was not distracted by the surroundings, but strode straight to the dome in the centre of the hall. Holding his ring up to the light, he soared up into the air. After remaining suspended in a halo of bright light for a while, he found himself falling gently back down like a feather in the wind. As he descended, the blinding light subsided and he found himself in a dark, cloudy recess of the eternal hall. Ahead of him was an archway floating above the ground which was marked 'To Bodleian Library.' Rupert walked through the archway and emerged in Oxford.

Quickly, he left the Bodleian and tried to find Urganda College without looking too much like an imposter. When somebody spoke to him, he was so alarmed that he jumped and the air around him felt as cold as ice.

'Hello!' A first-year student dressed in the same manner greeted Rupert cheerfully. 'I presume you are going to the celebrations at Urganda College tonight.'

'Oh, yes,' replied Rupert. 'I'm afraid I'm not very organised; do you happen to know when it starts?'

'Not exactly - I'm not very organised either - but we may as well go over now,' he led Rupert away from the Bodleian and into the old-fashioned quadrangle outside Urganda College. 'What's your name?'

'Bertie,' replied Rupert, this being the first name he thought of which was not his own.

'Charles. Nice to meet you,' they shook hands. 'So, what subject do you do?'

'Music,' said Rupert, thinking that it was highly unlikely that his new acquaintance also took this subject and would therefore catch him out, since he appeared, in his view, rather too normal to be a musician.

'Ah, what instrument do you play? Do you enjoy it? I don't think there are many of us in that department, are there?' Charles' well-meaning talkativeness was beginning to disconcert Rupert.

'No, there aren't many of us,' he remarked, 'but it's very nice indeed, much nicer than a music college. I did get offered a place at the Royal Academy - I play the violin, by the way - but I decided I'd rather come here for the lifestyle, and to be in the League, of course.' As they entered the college, Rupert felt himself growing more confident in his role. 'What subject do you take?'

'Classics,' said Charles. 'It's very exciting, actually. At my last tutorial, our tutor, who is a slightly eccentric wizard, was discussing the validity of the claim of St Augustine, that Apuleius' Golden Ass was based on his own experience. To demonstrate, he transformed himself into a donkey - a grey one, rather than golden, by the way - and at that moment, one of the other professors walked in. She doesn't know that he's a wizard, so imagine her surprise at seeing two students and a very scholarly-looking donkey! I told her our tutor had brought in his pet donkey and would be back in a minute. As she already considers him next door to a lunatic, she readily accepted the explanation.'

Despite the rather precarious position he was in, the anecdote amused Rupert so much that he laughed quite naturally, just as if he were not an imposter and Charles were his old friend. Upon entering the college, he promptly found himself engulfed by a crowd of students and swept along into the kitchen.

'What happens now?' asked Rupert.

'We have to take the canapés upstairs to serve before they go into the hall. Didn't you read the instructions?' one of the girls remarked.

'I'm glad you know what you're doing, Lucy,' said Charles. 'This is Bertie, by the way. He plays the violin and studies music here.'

'Really? Do you think you could summon the dead out of their graves?' she asked, suddenly interested.

'I don't know, I haven't tried,' replied Rupert, 'Anyone you would like me to summon in particular?'

'Not really, I just thought it would be interesting. I do think graveyards at midnight are lovely,' she tucked her hair behind her ears, not seeming to think she had made a strange remark at all. 'I imagine they'll be talking about politics as usual.'

'How very tedious,' remarked Charles.

'Not really,' replied Lucy, 'It's actually quite sensational these days. Haven't you heard the rumours that an ancient relic has been found?'

'Yes,' said Rupert, pricking up his ears. 'What do you think about it? Do you think we should release the spirit of Isolda?'

'I don't think it would be a very good idea at all, for it would be damaging for our relations with humans, and the vampires would probably interfere. They interfere with everything. Come on, it's time,' Lucy picked up a tray and they followed her upstairs.

'Oh, I concur,' replied Rupert. 'I think the policy of integration is a good thing.'

'Although we'll never be truly integrated, of course. We always seem to be a bit odd,' observed Charles. 'You know, I don't think humans would enjoy waking up the dead or such things, and they wouldn't be able to cope with their familiars bothering them all the time. Does yours bother you?'

'Oh yes, she's very bossy,' replied Rupert, 'but I think cats usually are. She tells me off if I don't practise violin diligently enough.'

At this point they separated, and Rupert meandered around the reception room, offering canapés to the witches and wizards as they arrived. As he hovered silently behind the various groups, he listened to the conversation and caught snippets of university gossip but nothing related to the relic. After he had sufficiently examined the ornately carved ceiling and Corinthian pillars, he began to feel a little disappointed at how ordinary the gathering was, and wandered over to talk to Charles, hoping to glean a little information.

'How are you getting on, Bertie?' he asked cheerfully and Rupert almost jumped as he had quite forgotten his assumed name. 'They'll be wanting wine now, so we may as well have a glass before it runs out - they won't mind.'

'No thanks,' said Rupert. 'Excuse me for a moment.'

He slipped quickly away from Charles and melted into the crowd, for at that moment his sharp ears had caught the name of Isolda. A group of wizards, mostly middle-aged, had entered and were engaged in an animated discussion, glancing furtively around to make sure they were not overheard. Rupert concealed himself behind a pillar and listened.

'What news from Isolda?' a tall, bearded man was asking.

'Not much,' replied another. 'She has reported that she is settling in well at St Jude's but has not yet been able to release the relic.'

'Are you sure she can be trusted with so important a mission?'

'Her loyalty is unquestionable. Even if she were to have doubts about the cause, her great attachment to Julius would silence them.'

'I wasn't questioning her loyalty so much as her abilities,' observed the bearded wizard condescendingly. 'I have always been dubious about entrusting too much to young girls: they are so emotional and often put such personal considerations before the greater good.'

'That is certainly often the case,' chimed in a third man with owlish spectacles, 'and she is by no means exempt from sudden afflictions of feeling. You will remember how when she first came here she was quite distraught by the death of her schoolfriend, who had witnessed her first attempt to obtain the relic - though she was a mere human girl whose death hardly mattered, Isolda was very emotional about it, quite unreasonably so.'

At this point, Rupert was quivering with excitement at the unexpected yield of his eavesdropping, but his blood ran cold at the callousness with which they discussed the death of Margaret.

The one who had mentioned Julius said, 'However, Julius is quite convinced that she is the chosen one, and he's usually right. Apparently, that girl who died has become a slightly troublesome ghost, but he has her under control. Julius also reports that a most irritating vampire boy and his friends are investigating the case, though of course they have not realised that Isolda has returned to her old school. Even her old teachers do not recognise her.'

Suddenly, one of the group who had not spoken hitherto caught sight of Rupert and called out sharply, 'Hello there, stop daydreaming and bring us a bottle of champagne, boy!'

Startled, Rupert swiftly obeyed and poured the effervescent wine into crystal champagne flutes with an elegance which would have pleased even Hawkins.

'Will that be all?' he asked politely.

'Yes, yes, thank you,' the peevish man waved him away dismissively. 'Are you sure that Julius has everything under control? After all, he does not live at St Jude's,' he continued, after ascertaining that Rupert had gone.

'Quite sure. He's only in the village at any rate and he visits Isolda often to check up on her.'

'Do you not think that might arouse suspicion?'

'By no means: it is not at all unusual for an attractive young woman to have a regular male visitor. Besides, not only does she require his instructions but she also adores his company.'

'I just wish they would make a little more progress,' said the bearded man impatiently. 'Already, there are rumours circulating among the students that the miniature has been found, so it is essential that we master its power before the authorities interfere. I hope they do know what they are doing and that our plans will not be thwarted by a boy and a ghost.'

'I am sure we have no cause for concern,' the one with the glasses reassured him. 'Julius has the ghost under control, and the boy is more of an irritant than a danger. He can easily be removed if necessary, but Julius has refrained from doing so in order not to cause superfluous conflict with the vampires.'

'Humph!' remarked the man who had ordered the champagne from Rupert.

However, whatever he intended to say after this eloquent comment was interrupted by the gong summoning the members into the Great Hall for dinner. Charles suddenly materialised at Rupert's elbow.

'Hello, old chap, how was it? I noticed you served the Bursar champagne and felt rather sorry for you, for he's terribly bad-tempered.'

'Indeed, he was rather,' replied Rupert absently.

'Are you alright? Come on, we need to hurry,' he squeezed through the throng and Rupert decided this would be a good time to make his exit.

With this in mind, he allowed the horde of members to surge past him. Overall, he felt it had been a very successful evening's work, though he was somewhat disturbed by the conversation of the extremist sector of the League. Stealthily, he glided out of the college like a ghost and made for the Bodleian. Darkness was entombing the world. Though he liked the dark normally, he felt a little on edge and the lights of the library were friendly and welcoming.

A few times, he turned round sharply, sensing that he was being followed. However, he could not see anyone, so he merely walked more briskly down the long path towards his destination.

Suddenly, as he approached the door, a dark figure pounced out of the shadows. Rupert recognised the Bursar looming over him. He tried to back away into the sanctuary of the Bodleian, but the heavy doors would not give way. The wizard raised his hand threateningly. Rupert bared his fangs and clutched his dagger.

'So, you have come here to spy on us!' the Bursar growled. 'My colleague is clearly mistaken when he suggests you do not need to be removed yet. I shall have to dispose of you before the soup is served.'

'I wouldn't try, if I were you,' said Rupert quietly, kicking the door with increasing frustration.

'The door will not open. You are all alone and vulnerable. It would be futile to put up a fight,' with these ominous words, the Bursar began muttering a spell in a thunderous voice.

Desperation seized Rupert. Without thinking, he flew at the Bursar. Surprised, the latter staggered backwards, gingerly feeling the cut on his cheek. However, he almost immediately continued his deadly incantation.

Suddenly, the doors of the Bodleian flew open with a wild gust of wind. Rupert at once plunged into the darkness of the library. He tried to slam them shut again, but at that moment, flames encircled him, blinding him with their light. The wizard promptly retreated, terrified by the blaze. Then the flames flickered and died, leaving Rupert in darkness amid the books. Just before the doors closed, he heard a voice calling the Bursar for the soup.

Breathing a sigh of relief, he turned and looked around him. To his surprise, he found himself in the company of a crimson dragon who enfolded him in her majestic wings affectionately.

'Lady Gwendolen!' he cried joyfully. 'This is a very fortunate coincidence: I really thought for a moment that I might die here, all alone. Thank you for rescuing me. Indeed, it was just in time.'

'You're quite welcome, Rupert,' she replied graciously, resuming the form of a lady, 'although it was not entirely a coincidence. Your mother, when she heard from the butler what was going on, asked me to keep an eye on you, so I took the opportunity to catch up with my Oxford friends.'

'I asked Hawkins to preserve the secrecy of my plans,' remarked Rupert. 'Put not your trust in butlers.'

Lady Gwendolen laughed, 'Well, fortunately for you, Hawkins did not consider himself bound to secrecy. Come along, I will escort you back to the castle. And do put that dagger away - it is rather bad manners to carry naked blades around ladies.'

Having thus admonished him, she blew a ring of flames around them and they were whisked straight to the castle in an incandescent swirl. When they arrived, Rupert's mother embraced him and kissed his forehead, which operation he humbly submitted to while his father looked on and smiled.

'Oh Rupert, you do cause me great anxiety at times,' she reproached him gently. 'I am too wise to forbid escapades of this sort - boys like adventures, and knowing your father, I am aware of the futility of prohibiting them, for you take after him. However, I should like to be informed about them in the future, by you rather than by Hawkins.'

'Yes, Mama,' said Rupert demurely. 'Overall, it was a very successful escapade, you know, although I was in a bit of an awkward situation when Lady Gwendolen found me.'

'To be precise, my dear Madeleine,' put in the dragon affably, 'he was being attacked by the Bursar of Urganda College, who is, as you know, a most dangerous radical. He was, at that moment, particularly incensed, because Rupert had just cut his cheek open, and had I not arrived, tragedy could have ensued.'

'Ah, I cannot thank you enough for looking out for him,' sighed Rupert's mother. 'Come into the drawing room and have some refreshment with us.'

Rupert's father chuckled, 'Well, Rupert, I am pleased that associating with all those um... nerds - I believe that is the correct term - at school has not made you effeminate, but I shall clearly have to give you fencing lessons.'

When they were all seated drinking tea in the drawing room, he gravely asked for an explanation of exactly what Rupert was up to, 'The other day, you know, I thought I sensed you in the castle, but then I realised you were in school. However, I found various ingredients missing from the laboratory.'

'Yes, I did take some things from the laboratory on Thursday,' explained Rupert. 'Did Lady Gwendolen tell you about the Book of Dreams? Well, Ada entered it and spoke to the author, who advised her to enter the mind of the ghost, Margaret. However, when she did this, a wizard was watching Margaret and when he saw what we were doing, he prevented Ada from seeing any more by making her faint. I borrowed the ingredients to make a potion which would cure her, and fortunately, the enchantment had no long-lasting ill effects.'

'Ah, so you then rather imprudently decided to enter the Oxford League of Witches.'

'Indeed, and I found out some valuable information. I learned from their conversation that Isolda has returned to St Jude's under an assumed identity in order to obtain the witch's miniature. There is a member of the League called Julius who apparently stays in the village, but visits her to give her instructions. It is he who reports to the extremist sect and I think he must be the man whom Margaret mentioned. The impression I got from the conversation is that Julius is Isolda's boyfriend; it seems that he is the real mastermind behind the plot, but is using her because he, for some reason, believes she is the chosen one. I can't think how the Bursar recognised me, but clearly Julius has been watching and reporting the progress of our investigations.'

Having finished making these revelations, Rupert put his teacup down emphatically. The Duke, seeing that some comment was expected of him, merely shook his head in a mildly disapproving kind of way.

'Rupert, what you have discovered is of a very serious nature. The Witches' Council should probably be informed at some point,' his mother remarked, in a tone of slight condescension towards that organisation. 'You see, if the miniature falls into the hands of extremists, it will give them the power to destroy the peace which has been painstakingly established between the species. We must be careful, for dark times may lie ahead.'

CHAPTER 12 - ISOLDA

As he lay in bed that night, Rupert's thoughts were like fragile ships tossed on a turbulent sea. The full moon gazed down at him through the window, softly bathing his face in silver light, as if he were a second Endymion. However, the caressing rays of the moon could not sooth him or lull him to sleep. In his mind, he pictured again and again the tragic death of Margaret. It seemed clear to him that Isolda had betrayed her friend, but how could he tell her? The thought of the lonely ghost haunting the archive, never at peace, almost brought tears to his eyes.

After a while, he drifted into a fitful sleep. His dreams were shadowy and full of confusion, but always overshadowed by the ominous figure of Julius, whoever he might be. Suddenly, he woke up with his heart pounding against his chest and his fists tightly clenched. The velvety darkness enveloped him and at length brought calm to his feverish mind.

No longer disposed to sleep, he began trying to analyse the case. The more he thought about it, the more inevitable his theory became. The wizards had said that Isolda had returned recently to St Jude's. The only new arrival at the school was the biology teacher, Miss Gourlay. She had been to Urganda College; she had seemed familiar with the school from the very start; Ada thought she had heard her voice before. All of these apparently insignificant things drew Rupert inexorably to the conclusion that Isolda and Miss Gourlay were one and the same. He wished that he might be mistaken, for he liked her as a teacher very much, but he knew in his heart that he was right. How could it be that the friendly biology teacher was involved in the plots of the League? How could she, who seemed so gentle and kind, be a murderer?

These thoughts haunted Rupert, so that he spent all the next day wandering about like a restless ghost, unable to settle down to anything. When he practised his violin, he felt he heard Margaret's melancholy singing. When he walked around the castle grounds and looked up at the bleak towers, he imagined her scream of terror as she fell. Even when he wrote to Rosaline to report on his adventure, while Hawkins was pottering around in the background, the shadow of the butler became sinister and took the form of the mysterious man who was always watching him at school.

On Monday, he told his friends all that had occurred over the weekend, as soon as they could be alone. Somehow, telling the story made it all seem less horrifying; it put some distance between himself and the events. He even rather enjoyed the others' expressions of horror when he described how he had been followed by the Bursar.

'You think that Isolda is Miss Gourlay? I can hardly believe it,' declared Bertie when he had finished.

'Nor could I, but it is the only logical conclusion,' replied Rupert. 'The point is, I would like to be certain, as she looks nothing like the picture of Isolda which we saw. Therefore, I propose we ask Margaret to follow her and identify her, for ghosts can always see past any disguises into a person's soul. In this way, we will also have a way of knowing what passes between her and Julius, for he is sure to visit soon.'

Ada remarked pensively, 'Don't you find it strange, Rupert, that we have never noticed this man before if he visits her so regularly?'

'Not at all, for we were never looking for him. Besides, what with rehearsals for the play and all those tests we've been having, we have had no leisure to observe all the visitors to the school. We will certainly need Margaret's help, because the performance is at the end of the week, so we shall have no time at all.'

'Poor Mr Beanacre,' observed Beatrice with a smile. 'Well, haven't you noticed he seems to actually enjoy talking to Miss Gourlay, though he normally can't stand socialising? I imagine his pleasant dreams would be shattered if he found out about Julius.'

'Good heavens, I had not thought of that!' cried Rupert.

'Wouldn't his dreams be more shattered if he found out she was a murderer?' put in Bertie.

'Are you sure it was her, though?' asked Ada dubiously.

'Well, not absolutely,' admitted Rupert, 'but who else could it be? All we need is evidence. Let's find Margaret first.'

The four friends hurried to the archive. This time, Margaret seemed to have been waiting for them, as she appeared at once. Rupert explained everything to her and she listened silently, though she turned even paler as he proceeded.

When he had finished, she exclaimed indignantly, 'Rupert, that is a preposterous idea! I can believe that Isolda was trying to release the witch's miniature, but I cannot believe that she killed me. I knew her better than anyone, and I know she would not betray me for anything.'

'But Margaret, you can't know that, because you don't remember your death properly,' pointed out Rupert. 'She had the motive and the opportunity.'

'And yet that does not make her guilty,' replied Margaret, and objected passionately to any further arguments which he could put forward against Isolda. 'However, I will follow her and tell you all that she does. I hope that when I have reported all this to you, Rupert, you will be convinced of her innocence, even though you have a tendency, like most boys, to always think you are correct.'

Much disturbed by all Rupert had said, Margaret faded into the air and the children hurried off to lessons. Meanwhile, he was rather perplexed, for her unshakable confidence in her friend had made him doubt his own theory. Yet he could not think of another more convincing explanation either, though he in fact hoped that Margaret was right. He discussed the matter with Ada, but this shed no light on the mystery, for she was certain that there had been no third person present when Margaret died, from what she had seen when she entered her memories.

As a result of this mental preoccupation, he only nodded absent-mindedly when Ernest consulted him on the no less difficult conundrum of Mr Mond's play. With the date of the performance impending, he was now troubled not only by people forgetting their lines, but also by the issue of the set. For the steam train scenes, they had at length decided against using year sevens to represent the train, in favour of a projected image on the wall. The only problem was that Mr Jury, though an excellent Latin teacher, had immense difficulty with modern technology and in his distress, considered the projector to be a form of witchcraft. Fortunately, he had plenty of time to devote to battling with it, for ever since the day when he had told Rupert about Margaret, his Colosseum had remained free of dust.

While the children were occupied in these and similar matters, Margaret set about following Miss Gourlay. Since she had previously been in hiding in the archive, she had not yet come across her in the school. As she tentatively ventured out of this sanctuary, her thoughts were in turmoil. Although she hoped to see Isolda again, at the same time she feared what she might discover. She wished ardently that the memory of her innocent childhood would not be shattered.

At first she was apprehensive, as she floated silently along the corridors, in case she was noticed. However, as nobody seemed aware of her presence, she soon grew more confident and began peeping into the rooms. She even felt a surge of bittersweet nostalgia warming her fragile, translucent form, as she overheard Mr Dodd humming to himself in the chapel or Mrs Johnson becoming enthusiastic about Priestley. Now an unknown child sat in the seat which had been hers, someone else sang in her old choir stall, but returning now to these places in the light of day felt like coming home, after so long alone in the darkness of the archive.

When she approached the science labs, she froze in her tracks. A voice drifted through the half-open door which made her tremble as though an icy hand had touched her heart. That voice brought back a flood of memories which overwhelmed her. In those melodious tones so familiar to her, the voice directed the class in the examination of onion cells under a microscope, in a way which somehow made this seem like a divine revelation.

Breathlessly, Margaret peeped through the door and stared at her. It was Isolda; her golden hair had changed to ebony and her eyes too were chestnut rather than blue, but there could be no mistake about it. Margaret saw past these superficial changes into her soul. At that moment, any doubts which Rupert had sown in her mind dissolved and she felt only joy at being with her friend once more.

While Isolda taught her lessons and chatted in the staffroom with the teachers who knew her under another identity, Margaret followed her at a distance. She did not materialise, lest she were seen, but drifted along with her, as insubstantial as the air itself. When evening came, Isolda went for a walk, followed by her ghostly companion. When they passed the castle, she gazed up at the tower and sighed. Briskly, she walked on towards the river that ran by the school.

The night wind lamented in the trees and in the reeds which huddled together on the riverbank. A few stars glimmered in the sky, but they were timid and frequently veiled themselves behind wispy grey clouds. Isolda bent down to gather some mysterious herbs. As the moon sailed out of the clouds for a moment, Margaret saw that a few strands of her hair had turned blonde. Crushing the herbs in her hands, she murmured an incantation, and her hair became raven black once more. Having completed the renewal of her disguise, she made her way rather listlessly back to the school.

As Margaret hovered behind her, she was filled with anxiety for her friend. She was just the same as when they were at school in some ways, yet in others she was a complete stranger. When she was performing her spells, cloaked in the secretive darkness, she had seemed wild and strange, like a Medea, thought Margaret. Nothing could be further from the innocent girl she had known. However, the deep sadness, which had clouded her beautiful features when she passed the castle, was all too familiar. She remembered how

Isolda as a child had wept floods of tears over the separation of her parents, how desperately she had tried to be the daughter her mother wanted and longed for the loving embraces of a father. When she visited Margaret in the holidays, she had observed her friend's idyllic family life with a kind of awe, as though this were quite unfamiliar to her. As Margaret floated back into the archive, it was the memories of Isolda which were tinged with melancholy that appeared in her mind's eye.

The next morning, she continued shadowing her at a safe distance, but nothing of interest happened until the afternoon. As she had a free period, she retired to her room in Old School House and did some marking. However, her expression was troubled and she made green ticks haphazardly over the exercise books without really comprehending what she was reading. This went on for about a quarter of an hour when Margaret heard heavy footsteps on the stairs, followed by the pattering steps of the receptionist.

'There's a gentleman to see you, Miss Gourlay,' she called.

'Oh, thank you, please show him in,' she replied absently.

A moment later, a man whom Margaret did not recognise entered the room, closing the door softly behind him. He was of middling height and would have been handsome if his face were not permanently severe in its expression. Although he could not have been older than thirty, his brow was already creased with several marked lines. His eyes were sharp and piercing, but they were the one feature which did not appear as formidable as the rest: whenever they settled on anything, they looked as if they were seeking something elusive beyond it but were not quite sure what they were seeking. This, thought Margaret, must be the boyfriend whom Rupert mentioned, though her taste must have changed, for in sixth form such a man would never have been attractive to Isolda.

'Hello, Isolda,' said the man, in a rather restrained way, almost shy. 'Ah, I see you are very conscientious about your job. What is it like, teaching biology to the pupils of a second-rate private school, when you could be doing so much more?'

'It's alright,' she replied, without looking up from her work. 'I actually quite enjoy it, apart from the marking; the sound of childish laughter is remarkably soothing when my mind is so often occupied by dark and serious subjects. Why have you come?' she asked abruptly after a moment.

He paced around the room, 'The League told me to check up on you again, that's all. You don't need to be touchy about me, you know. I told them that I'm sure you just need time, but they are beginning to want results before the other part of the League start poking their noses in. But Isolda, try not to lose sight of what is at stake.'

'I'm not. I have been trying.'

'Yes, of course you have, and of course I appreciate your efforts,' he assured her with a kind of awkward gentleness, as if this were alien to him usually. 'It's just that the Bursar is afraid your - how shall I put it

– personal connections with this place may make you prone to - er - sentimentality, which might mean you are not fully committed.'

'Sentimentality!' cried Isolda indignantly. 'Is it sentimentality to remember every time I pass the castle that my best friend died there? Is is sentimentality to be constantly gnawed by guilt because she would not have died had her concern for me not prompted her to follow me on that fateful day? I know you call it collateral damage, a small sacrifice for our cause, but you would not say that if you had known her. Yet for all my sentimentality, as the Bursar calls it, I will deliver the miniature to him. I have never wavered from this goal, not even when, standing on the tower, I hear in my imagination her scream as she fell. I feel that the spirit is awakening and beginning to respond more favourably to my summons. In a few days, perhaps even tomorrow, I will call her again, and I believe I will succeed. Now, I think you had better report back to the League, and I had better get on with my marking.'

Thoroughly subdued by this speech, the man hastily said goodbye and left. Margaret half wanted to reveal herself and comfort her, but she reflected that it would be better to find out who this man was, so she followed him down to reception, always at a safe distance. When he had signed out and left, she noticed that the name on the register was Julius.

One of the receptionists asked the other, 'Who was that man?'

'He came to see Miss Gourlay,' she replied. 'A friend from Oxford, apparently.'

'Oh, well that must be nice for her. She doesn't socialise very much, so it's a good thing her friend came to see her, or she might get lonely living alone in the school.'

Then they spoke of other matters, and Margaret drifted away, having decided to relay all this to the children. However, as they were still in lessons, she did not get a chance to do so, but meandered back to the archive to ponder on what she had seen and heard. She was much intrigued by the strange man and wondered how it could be that he had such great influence over Isolda, whom she considered to be a victim of the manipulation of the League. With these and other conjectures, she whiled away the time until evening drew a veil over the school.

Meanwhile, as Margaret had been observing this scene, the children were in a physics lesson. Due to the eccentricities of the physics teacher, these were usually quite eventful, and today even more than usual. Mr Beanacre was not in his most jovial mood, and was in fact growing increasingly irate, because he had achieved the lowest average mark out of the three classes in the recent test, despite the fact that he had written it. As he expressed his displeasure at this result, which had greatly embarrassed him in the staffroom, he marched up and down in front of the class, gesticulating wildly. Even the seven clocks shuddered into ticking more quietly, lest they bring his wrath down upon themselves.

The class was also very subdued, for the children were not accustomed to such explosions from any other teachers. However, Mr Beanacre was very ambitious about all his classes, despite his inability to teach them effectively, and therefore felt it to be a blow to his honour and reputation if they did not out-perform the classes of the other two physics teachers. Indeed, this tendency towards pushing his pupils to achieve in a somewhat aggressive manner caused some distress to Dr Botherby, who felt it was against his educational principles, and to Mr Mond, who thought it might lead to psychological issues.

'It is absolutely disgraceful that my class average was the lowest of the three!' he cried. 'After all, what was the point in having Rupert and Ada in my class to get the top marks in the year group when I also have so many people who failed that my average was brought down so much?'

While he continued grumbling, the girl sitting next to Bertie demanded to see his paper, then remarked indignantly, 'I don't know how you managed to do so much better than me.'

'Well, I revised very thoroughly, Becky,' he replied mildly. 'I'm sure you'll do better next time.'

She haughtily gazed down her sharp nose at him, 'Well, even if you did swot for the test, I was copying you, so I can't understand why that happened. Ada, what did you get?'

'Ninety-seven per cent,' she replied. 'Same as Rupert, but it was a different mark that he dropped.'

Becky said, 'Of course, I should have known. You always do well on the tests nobody else does well on. But Bertie, how is it that you only got eighty-three?'

'I was feeling quite pleased with my eighty-three,' remarked Bertie.

'Oh, it's good for you,' she said contemptuously, 'but you could have copied better than that.'

'Copied?' Bertie's eyes widened and he said in an injured tone, 'But I wasn't copying Ada! I have integrity you know.'

'You weren't? Well, you should have told me. I would never have copied you if I'd known it was actually your own work!' she turned away haughtily.

Bertie was left speechless by this last remark. However, being of a cheerful disposition, a sympathetic look from Ada promptly restored his high spirits. The same could hardly be said for Mr Beanacre, who even when he had finished grumbling, appeared nervous and irritable. During the remainder of the lesson, he bounced over to one or other of the clocks and glared at it so frequently, that Rupert began to wonder what he was waiting for so anxiously.

'Rupert, has it ever occurred to you that Becky is a very annoying person?' asked Bertie afterwards.

Rupert laughed, 'Certainly, but I rarely pay attention to her. We have more important things to consider: I'm sure Margaret will discover something soon.'

That evening, the four children gathered in the common room of St Cecelia's house after rehearsals. The weather had become too cold, with a hint of frost embroidering the grass outside, to sit on the bench outside the music department at this time. However, the common room was always so noisy and bustling that they were as secluded as if they were alone. They passed the time by discussing the play and other trivial matters, but all of them felt a growing sense of impatient curiosity, hoping that Margaret would appear, for they would not be able to slip into the archive while under the benevolent but vigilant supervision of Mrs Johnson.

Presently, Rupert felt a cold touch on his shoulder. Ada's face lit up as she saw Margaret, who was hovering behind him, invisible to all except the two of them. Rupert smiled to himself, pleased that Ada's supernatural gifts seemed to have developed, allowing her to see the ghost clearly. He was not quite sure why this pleased him; perhaps it made him feel she was more like him. Without turning around, he greeted Margaret silently and asked her what she had discovered. She telepathically communicated this to him before drifting away quickly, to continue her secret observation of Isolda.

'Did she come? What did she say?' asked Beatrice, sensing that Rupert had suddenly become more animated.

'She said I was right about Isolda,' he whispered, his green eyes flashing like a cat's in the dark. 'She is really Miss Gourlay. Apparently, a man named Julius visited her today and told her on behalf of the League to hurry up and get the miniature. She told him off but said she thinks she will succeed in the next few days.'

'Do you still think she was the murderer?' asked Ada.

'I don't know,' he frowned, resting his chin on his

hand. 'Margaret is convinced of her innocence, and the fact is, I think she's far too nice to be guilty. However, we must not allow personal feelings to influence this case, and I still can't think who else it could be. What do you think?'

'I feel instinctively that it was not her, or at least not her alone,' replied Ada. 'You see, when I entered Margaret's memories, she was always standing in front of Margaret, never behind, so she could not have pushed her off the tower.'

'She wouldn't need to be behind her,' pointed out Rupert, 'because you can kill someone without physically touching them, by controlling their mind momentarily, so that they jump themselves in a fit of madness.'

'That's all very well, but I have a second reason for thinking there were two people there with Margaret. I know I did not actually see anyone else, but I have been turning this over in my mind many times, and something else has occurred to me. Just before I fainted, I felt like I was falling off the tower myself, and above me there were confused shadows and voices - the voices of two people, Isolda and a man - but I don't know what they were saying.'

'Do you think it was the man who visited her today? He could have been at the school then; we just assumed she met him afterwards,' suggested Beatrice.

Rupert pondered, 'There's something not right about this man. I just can't quite place it. Margaret said she had never seen him before, and by their conversation, I wouldn't have thought they were very close. He didn't behave at all like a boyfriend.'

'So, is this man not the same one who has been interfering with our investigations here?' asked Bertie.

'No, she was quite adamant about that. I don't see how there could be two men involved,' Rupert was puzzled. 'The other strange thing is that he hasn't been here before - the receptionist didn't recognise him - but I know from what I heard at the festival of Hecate that he visits her often, although he lives in the village.'

The others were equally baffled. For a few minutes they remained silent, plunged in thought.

A voice pierced Rupert's contemplations from one of the other groups of children, 'Do you know, I have to wear one of those weird, feminine hats with big plumes for Mr Mond's play? Thankfully, Mrs Johnson said I didn't absolutely have to wear tights, or stockings, or whatever they are that men used to wear, if I couldn't get hold of any. Really, it's just typical of Mr Mond to write a play set centuries ago and make the costumes so strange.'

Suddenly, Rupert cried, 'Of course!' exultantly.

The other three looked at him in surprise and he explained more quietly, 'There is one element we have not yet considered: Mr Mond's play. Do you remember what Mr Mond said to Ernest? That when he was writing the play, he decided to insert the school legend and also wrote another scene involving the witch's descendant, the second Isolda, searching for the miniature, and that he had planned to put a murder in, but all of a sudden the idea had left him. Doesn't the plot of Act Four of Mr Mond's play seem uncannily similar to this case?'

'Gosh, I'd never have thought of that!' said Bertie. 'What exactly are you suggesting?'

'That Mr Mond accidentally hit upon the truth in his attempt to write something sensational; the man made his mind go blank to avoid this. He must live near Mr Mond, who we know lives in the village, near the Cathedral. Otherwise, he would not have known what Mr Mond was writing, for he always writes in the holidays.'

'Which man do you mean, though?'

'There is only one man who matters, the real Julius, not the one who visited Miss Gourlay today - he is irrelevant. I am referring to the mastermind behind the whole plot involving the miniature, the man who is so anxious to stop our investigations because he is the murderer.'

'But who is it?' they demanded.

'I'm not completely sure, because this is going to sound absolutely ridiculous, but I think…'

At that moment, Mrs Johnson bustled over and admonished Rupert and Bertie, 'Now, boys, I know you enjoy the company of Ada and Beatrice, so I have ignored the fact that you should be in your own house, but as I am about to send everyone to bed, you really must leave now. Good night,' she said majestically.

The boys obediently rushed to St Anthony's house just as the bell was sounding for bed. Bertie, burning with curiosity, kept pressing Rupert to reveal his suspicions as they undressed, but he refused, saying he needed time to think his theory through. He hoped that soon, whenever Isolda tried to release the spirit again, his instincts would be confirmed. Despite being left in ignorance of his friend's thoughts, Bertie promptly fell into a contented sleep. In the next bed, Rupert lay with his eyes closed but his mind fully awake and buzzing with anticipation.

CHAPTER 13 - THE WITCH'S MINIATURE

Solemnly, the Cathedral bells struck midnight. The school was shrouded in deathly silence, except for the haunting reverberations of those bells. Exhausted, Rupert at last dropped into a deep, dreamless sleep.

It seemed to him that only a few minutes had passed, when he was abruptly awakened by a ghostly presence at the end of his bed. He glanced sleepily at the clock. It was half past four in the morning. The night was stubbornly clinging on to the world, but the blackness had faded into grey: dawn was approaching. In the trees outside, a few sprightly birds were already beginning to try out their voices in the frosty air.

'Margaret, what's going on?' he inquired silently.

'Get out of bed, Isolda is going to the castle this minute to acquire the witch's miniature,' she replied urgently. 'Otherwise, I assure you, I would not have entered one of the boys' dormitories for anything.'

Immediately, Rupert sprang out of bed, threw on his blazer over his pyjamas and slipped into his shoes.

The last vestiges of sleep were promptly dispelled as he hurried downstairs, as silent as a ghost himself. Margaret hovered in front of him, urging him to hurry. In the cold, grey dawn, the whole school seemed like a graveyard, filled with the lament of the whistling wind.

Suddenly, Rupert slowed down. Ahead of him, he glimpsed the figure of Isolda, purposefully approaching the castle. He followed her stealthily, quivering with excitement and apprehension. As they drew nearer, his sharp eyes glimpsed the shadow of a man standing on top of the tower. Isolda did not seem to be expecting him, for she made an irritated gesture with her head as she climbed the spiral staircase. Lingering in the shadows for a moment, Rupert made himself invisible, then dashed up the stairs after her.

When he saw who the man was, his first feeling was of joy that his deductions had been correct. This was rapidly succeeded by a sensation of horror. Beside him, Margaret almost faded away in shock.

'I hope you will succeed this time,' growled Mr Beanacre.

'I believe I will,' she replied, 'but I wish you would be a little more patient.'

'I haven't been impatient at all!' he retorted. 'I have been waiting for years for the moment when I can unleash the power of this ancient relic.'

'I know, I know,' she said, with a hint of weariness in her voice. 'But having you here inspecting me is very disconcerting. You don't seem to trust me any more, or I'm sure you would not have allowed the Bursar to send someone to check on me.'

She sounded so plaintive as she said this that Rupert was filled with sympathy for her. The wind crescendoed into an anguished howl, blowing a few strands of silky hair over her face. Her expression all of a sudden was helpless, pleading. Mr Beanacre remained as impassive as a rock.

'Why don't you trust me any more?' she asked falteringly.

'Don't be a silly girl,' he replied brusquely. 'I am just trying to impress you with a sense of urgency: I have discovered that the Witches' Council is watching us and knows about our plans. If I have the miniature, I will be able to seize power before it is too late, but if I don't get it soon, my career is over. As for the surprise visit, that was more intended for the ghost of Margaret than for you.'

'Whatever do you mean?' she cried, turning pale.

'Knowing how emotional and unreasonable you are about her, I didn't think it was a good idea to inform you that her ghost haunts the school and has been reporting on your movements to Rupert for the last three days.'

'Rupert?' she echoed. 'What's he got to do with it?'

'Well, he's a vampire,' he began.

'Yes, I know that! He's also very good at biology and a very nice, harmless sort of boy.'

'Nice, harmless sort of boy!' cackled Mr Beanacre. 'That's just where you're wrong, my dear. His father and mother are important members of the Vampire Liberal Party, and they both used to work for intelligence. Some of their nosiness has clearly rubbed off on their son! Do you know, he actually infiltrated the festival of Hecate and eavesdropped on our plans? Such foolish daring! Then again, it was in keeping with his character, for he once actually corrected me in one of my lessons,' he cried, growing increasingly angry.

'Well, you do make rather a lot of mistakes,' she pointed out mildly.

'Well, what do you expect? Chemistry is my subject; since it is a bit like making potions, I can actually teach that, but Dr Botherby asked me to teach physics as part of his ridiculous educational theory. Anyway, to return to the point: my rather obtuse colleagues didn't even notice that he wasn't one of the students until they had already committed quite a few indiscretions. It was the Bursar who saw through his disguise and tried to mislead him during the rest of the conversation, and he warned me to keep an eye on him. Anyway, the silly boy had got it into his head that you had a boyfriend who was giving you instructions. So when I discovered that he had asked Margaret to follow you and had guessed your true identity, I told them up at Oxford to send a young man to pose as said boyfriend, thereby confirming his theory and diverting any possible suspicions from myself. What's the matter with you now, Isolda?' he demanded, seeing her turn pale.

'Nothing, nothing,' she stammered, but her eyes were wide and vacant like a corpse's eyes. 'It's just that I can never forget Margaret's death, and for a moment I thought I saw her, accusing me with her dead eyes.'

'What nonsense!' cried Mr Beanacre. 'There, there,

don't distress yourself so much, little one,' he added, patting her arm with an air of tenderness that grated on Rupert's nerves. 'It was five years ago: there's nothing you can do about it now. Now, for goodness' sake, get on with summoning the spirit!'

Isolda walked slowly to the edge of the tower. Closing her eyes, she sank into a trance. Rupert watched her curiously as she began murmuring strange incantations, in an ethereal hum. The wind howled like a madman in the trees, tossing and turning in torment.

Suddenly, thunder roared overhead and a flash of lightning slashed through the sky. Mr Beanacre hopped up and down on his toes exultantly. The ground trembled and groaned, filling Rupert with a sense of awe. Quickly, he sent a telepathic message flying to his parents: come at once, the relic is being released.

Isolda continued with her incantations, waving her arms wildly. With a final piercing cry, her eyes flew open. A chasm burst open beneath the tower. In a cloud of dust and dark smoke, the miniature rose up from the depths of the earth. The golden frame glistened like fire. A pair of deep, blue eyes, passionate and mysterious, stared out of the picture. Rupert was struck by the magnetic beauty of the young witch, with her shining, golden hair and crimson lips, parted in a seductive smile.

Timidly, Isolda reached out to it, and the miniature floated towards her. In a burst of dazzling light, the form of her ancestor flew out of the confines of the frame and hovered before her in the sky. From what he had heard about her, Rupert was expecting her to appear bitter and vengeful, but as she extended her hands to Isolda, her expression was more of pathos than anger.

'At last, I am free from the odious confinement of this picture, free at last from the dull, clinging earth,' she sighed. 'Do not be afraid, dear child. My prophecy has been fulfilled: you, my descendant, have released my spirit, and you alone shall be my partner in greatness.'

At this juncture, Mr Beanacre leapt forward and tried to snatch the miniature.

However, the witch's spirit rebuked him forcefully, 'I have no intention of being commanded by a man - all men are hateful to me, except for the memory of the one man I loved. I see him now, so young and brave and foolish: I knew he would not be strong enough to resist my husband's savage fury, but he insisted on drawing his sword against him. The poor boy died in a pool of his own crimson blood, his lips still warm with my passionate kisses. And I was helpless to save him, for the whole world was against us: all the most powerful wizards in league with that domestic tyrant. When I saw my lover dying, still as handsome as a god and whispering my name with his last breath, I vowed that I would be avenged. Between them, these men drained the life out of me and they blackened my name for all posterity. I was unnatural, an aberration of nature, for I, a mere woman, was once a more accomplished sorcerer than all these men. Therefore I shall not use my powers to assist one man in overthrowing other men. You are all the same, driven only by cold ambition. Though it was your idea, I have chosen Isolda, not you.'

Despite his excitement almost amounting to madness, there was something compelling in her words which silenced him. However, when she had finished speaking, he turned on Isolda angrily.

'You are betraying me!' he cried accusingly. 'All those times you said you cared only for my aims to be fulfilled - you have forgotten now what you said then. Now you would rather have the power of the relic yourself. I really can't understand why you would prefer her to me: I am much more powerful,' he addressed the spirit again, ignoring Isolda's hurt expression.

'Indeed, you are at the moment, but you have reached the height of your powers and will develop no further, whereas I can see that she will in time supersede you by far. Besides, you are also too demanding,' she replied haughtily.

Mr Beanacre uttered a cry of disgust and outrage, 'All my plans have been ruined by you, Isolda!'

She clung to his arm beseechingly, 'Father, what are you saying? I have always loved you, always granted your every request. I will gladly give you the relic, but you must give me your love: that is all I want, all I ever longed for as a child, when you were a stranger to me. What does this relic matter? What do your political ambitions matter? I only cared about them to please you. All that matters to me is our family: you and mother and me, together and happy at last. Here, take the relic if it pleases you, but if you were to follow my advice, I would advise you to forget politics and enjoy life.'

The last words faded away in tears. Rupert was so shocked he was momentarily unable to move or think. Mr Beanacre was her father! It seemed almost impossible. The spirit of the Lady Isolda was visibly moved, but Mr Beanacre remained severely silent.

'My dear child, the relic is yours to receive but not to give,' the spirit began. 'Your filial affection is very touching, but...'

These words seemed to precipitate a minor explosion within the mind of Mr Beanacre. He leapt several feet into the air, uttering a cry of rage. Isolda shied away like a startled deer, gazing at him pleadingly. Just as Rupert was wondering when his parents were going to appear and what was taking them so long, Mr Beanacre lunged savagely at her.

'Father!' she cried, terrified. 'What madness has seized you? Am I not still your beloved daughter?'

Margaret uttered a horrified gasp, looking at Rupert for reassurance. Mr Beanacre, ignoring her tragic pleading, pushed his daughter roughly against the stone battlements. Eyes glinting ferociously, he bore down on her like a tiger upon a helpless doe.

Rupert threw himself between them, fists clenched, fangs bared, the hot blood rushing to his pale cheeks, 'Don't come near her!' he cried passionately.

'Rupert, what are you doing here?' she stammered.

Before he could reply, Mr Beanacre aimed a blow

at his head. For a moment, the whole world spun dizzily. There was such a dreadful cacophony, so much confusion. Awkwardly, he put his hands out to soften the fall and pain shot through him as he tumbled onto the hard granite. He scrambled to his feet and charged blindly, but was knocked down again. Now Mr Beanacre appeared like a giant, though this had never occurred to him during any physics lessons.

'Father!' shrieked Isolda. 'You must not hurt him, he is only a boy, I am begging you.'

Mr Beanacre cackled, imitating her voice, '"Father, I am begging you!" For a boy who is nothing to you! Why, he is only your pupil. He is old enough to meddle in my affairs, therefore he is quite old enough to face the consequences. Why are you looking at me in that sentimental way? You seem to think that because I am your father I am somehow bound to you by ties of family, of love. Silly girl - I was never a family man, never wanted a child so that I could experience the dubious joys of parenting. I leave that to mediocre wizards. The whole purpose of your existence, the very reason you were born, was to fulfil my ambition to acquire this relic, which had for so long eluded me. And this is the result! I renounce you, you are no longer my daughter!' blinded by fury, he rushed at her, as she burst into a flood of tears.

During this tirade, Rupert had managed to orient himself once more, despite feeling like someone was hammering the inside of his head. He wished he was taller, stronger. As it was, there was no way he could win this fight; he just had to hold out until his father arrived. Where on earth was he? All these thoughts flashed across his mind in a fraction of a second. He muttered an incantation under his breath, and flames danced in his hands. As Mr Beanacre was about to push Isolda off the parapet, he hurled the ball of fire at him. It missed narrowly, but he felt the heat on one side of his face, and wheeled round to confront Rupert like an enraged bull.

This time Rupert was ready for him. The heat of the moment had banished fear from his mind, and even the pain in his head was dulled. Dodging another blow to the head, he rushed at his opponent, slamming his fists into his stomach. Mr Beanacre groaned with pain, and involuntarily, Rupert smiled with a sort of savage pleasure, which the next moment left him confused and a little taken aback.

'I'll kill you!' cried Mr Beanacre, lunging at him wildly.

'And say it was suicide, like when you killed Margaret?' he shouted back, stepping quickly aside.

Mr Beanacre froze in his tracks.

'Father, please say it's not true! It can't be true!' wailed Isolda.

'Oh, can't it?' cried Rupert. 'For goodness' sake, don't be blinded by your longing for affection. Just now he tried to kill you, his own daughter: he is capable of anything. I know all about it now. I know how he followed you the day Margaret discovered your secret, how he sneaked up behind her and took control of her mind to make her throw herself from this tower, and afterwards how he lied about it to you and the whole world. I must confess that for a long time I suspected you, and he certainly had no scruples about confirming your guilt in my eyes for a crime you did not commit. Well, can you deny any of this, sir?' he added ironically.

'On the contrary, I deny none of it,' replied Mr Beanacre coldly. 'Your friend Margaret had discovered my plans, so she had to die. I knew you would be unreasonably upset over a mere human girl, so I concealed it from you. Rupert knows everything, therefore it is even more imperative that he must die.'

He began to recite a deadly incantation. Rupert panicked. He felt like he was being suffocated. There was nowhere to run. Suddenly, a flash of light dazzled his eyes, as his father materialised out of the air.

Hastily, he muttered something unintelligible which neutralised the curse of Mr Beanacre. Rupert breathed a sigh of relief. His father stood protectively in front of him and drew his sword. The first rays of the rising sun made it glint like fire, and his eyes too were fiery.

'So, you did come at last, to rescue your imbecile of a son, your Grace,' remarked Mr Beanacre disdainfully. 'Very well, then I shall have to kill you too.'

He also drew a sharp sword from out of the air. Grimly, the duellists began to circle each other. Rupert felt his breath catching in his throat with apprehension. A minute later, there was a rush of wind, as a group of witches and wizards on broomsticks swooped down onto the tower.

Suddenly, Isolda uttered a piercing cry. Everyone

turned and stared at her. Her eyes were deep pools of blue, and the black pupils seemed to be drowned in them. Without anybody noticing, the spirit of her ancestor, who had been hovering in the air, had descended onto her in an aureole of light. Isolda had undergone a metamorphosis: she now resembled in every detail the image of her ancestor. Her hands convulsively clutched the miniature as she glanced around feverishly, as if in a flight of madness.

Nobody quite liked to approach her, for they all realised that she had been possessed by the relic. However, this did not deter Mr Beanacre. By this point, he seemed to have completely taken leave of his senses. Brushing Rupert's father aside, he charged at her, brandishing his sword wildly. Without a word, she extended one hand, and blue flames shot from her fingers. Mr Beanacre was thrown backwards violently by the force of her magic, which had been strengthened so greatly by the spirit.

Seeing her father fall, a look of horror spread over her face and the madness vanished from her eyes for a moment, 'Please, leave me alone,' she murmured.

'Quickly, we must get the spirit back into the picture before she is completely possessed!' cried Rupert's father, taking charge.

Immediately, one of the wizards tried to grab the miniature, but as soon as he approached, he too was thrown backwards against the battlements. The spirit leapt back out of Isolda's body. Furiously, she attacked all the men present indiscriminately. Sparks flew everywhere. Everyone was thrown into a state of panic.

'Give me the miniature!' cried Rupert.

Hastily, Isolda thrust it into his hands, and he gave it to one of the witches, who appeared to be in charge. She ordered the others to all join hands, and they all began chanting a spell. A cry of despair tore through the air. The spirit of Lady Isolda vanished from the sky, trapped in the miniature. They produced a strangely carved wooden box, into which they placed the relic, sealing it with more powerful enchantments. Isolda stared vacantly at it for a moment, then fainted away.

Mr Beanacre remained indecisive for a moment. He felt that all was lost. With the ferocious madness of desperation, he lunged once more at Rupert's father, who parried deftly.

'Duke, we have no time for duelling!' the witch in charge admonished him, disarming Mr Beanacre with a wave of her hand. 'John, George, take him into custody, and put the miniature safely in the secret vault while you're about it. Off you go!'

The two wizards thus addressed took the no longer resisting Mr Beanacre into custody and flew off promptly on their broomsticks.

'Father!' Isolda, coming round from her faint, extended her arms upwards in a gesture of tragic despair.

Mr Beanacre did not even look back at her.

'There, there,' said Rupert's father, feeling that somebody ought to say something, but he coughed apologetically when he realised that this was not the right thing to say.

'I can't believe it,' she said, half to herself. 'I can hardly believe that he killed Margaret, and yet he confessed to it himself. How will I live without him? Of course,' she continued in a state of confusion, the words tumbling over each other, 'he is a murderer, so it is better that I should be without him, but he is still my father. Do you understand? He wasn't always like this, you know. Once, he was gentle and kind. It is the relic which has ruined and corrupted him, which has ruined me too. Alas, poor Margaret. If only she were with us now…'

At that moment, Margaret could no longer bear to remain hidden. She revealed herself to everyone and embraced Isolda, who stared at her in awe.

'Don't cry,' she said soothingly. 'Now my soul is at peace. Without him here suppressing me, my memories have all of a sudden become clear. Everything happened as Rupert said. However, it is now time to put the past behind us. You must embark upon a new life, Isolda, just as I must: I no longer have any desire to linger as a ghost, so I shall soon descend to the House of Death. You are not to blame for what has happened, so do not allow regret to haunt you. Rather, I want you to remember me cheerfully, as when I was alive. Rupert, thank you for setting me at rest; believe me, I am grateful to you all. Goodbye.'

A moment later, her silvery form dissolved into the air, leaving a silky trace gleaming in the rising sun. Deeply moved, they all preserved a reverent silence.

Rupert's mother, who had arrived with the

witches, embraced him lovingly, 'My poor, darling boy. Will you ever cease worrying me into premature old age?'

'I'll try, Mama, but I can't promise,' he laughed, inhaling the perfume in the folds of her dress with a sense of profound contentment.

The witch who was in charge remarked, 'It seems we arrived just in time. I really cannot express how grateful I am to you for warning us about the imminent release of the relic. Are you alright?' she peered at Rupert anxiously.

'Yes, thank you, quite well, now that everything has been sorted out.'

'Well, I'm glad to hear it, though you don't look very well at all: your left eye is turning a strange colour and looks rather swollen,' the witch informed him.

'Oh dear, does it look very bad? I need to look handsome for the play, you know,' he explained, somewhat flustered, while all the adults chuckled good-humouredly.

His mother put a thin layer of ointment over his eye, then wiped it off tenderly with a handkerchief. When this operation was completed, no trace of injury remained and the pain vanished immediately.

Rupert breathed a sigh of relief, 'Thanks, Mama. By the way, whatever took you so long, Papa?'

'Trying to get through the bureaucracy. The witches are a dreadfully bureaucratic people, you know, not like us. Your mother managed to finally impress them with the importance of the issue so that we were allowed to speak to the relevant people.'

'My dear,' said his wife, giving him a significant look, 'vampires are tolerably bureaucratic as well, but you haven't noticed, because you are one of the bureaucrats. Now, Rupert, you had better sneak back into the dormitory before anybody notices your absence and panics. We will arrange everything, and we'll see you for the play tomorrow.'

Following her advice, he ran down the spiral staircase, enjoying the pale yellow sunshine, which was not yet too strong. When he reached the bottom, he looked up and saw Miss Gourlay waving to him, as the witches led her gently away. He waved back and smiled, then slipped quietly back into St Anthony's house.

Later in the day, he told his friends about the dramatic events of the night. They listened with bated breath and wide eyes. Ada in particular was very anxious when he recounted the danger he had been through. He thought he saw her looking at him more tenderly than usual, and his heart thrilled within him. It was certainly worth it, just for that, he thought.

However, they did not spend as much time together discussing the case as he would have liked, for the girls were busy with their dress rehearsal and performance of Mr Mond's play, which was a resounding success. Rupert and Bertie went to see it, along with many other children from the other two houses, and they did not find it lacking in novelty by any means, for by the time Mrs Johnson had finished interpreting it, it was almost a different play. Indeed, Mr Mond was somewhat surprised but gratified by how literary it was.

'I hope ours goes just as well tomorrow, but somehow I don't think it will,' remarked Bertie afterwards.

Straight after breakfast the next day, an atmosphere of chaos began to make itself felt in St Anthony's house. During the dress rehearsal, Ernest attempted to remain calm and optimistic in the face of technological disasters, people falling over the set and one of the footmen breaking a plate during the banquet scene. However, his patience reached the limit when the boy returned without his costume after he had sent him to get a replacement plate from the kitchens.

'Sebastian, what have done with your tailcoat?' he asked exasperatedly.

'Dr Botherby confiscated it!' explained Sebastian. 'He said that he is going to be more strict about uniform, and that I had no right to wear it in the corridor, as it was not a school coat.'

'Good heavens! What a lot of fuss over nothing,' cried Ernest. 'Would you be able to persuade him not to disrupt our rehearsal in this manner, sir?'

Mr Jury pondered, then replied, 'I can try. I really don't know why he is doing this today, for he did not bother Mrs Johnson at all.'

'Well, nobody ever bothers Mrs Johnson without a very good reason. Really, Mr Jury, you ought to assert yourself,' remarked Ernest.

Thus encouraged, Mr Jury marched to the office of the Head of Academics and asked to know the reason for his confiscating the footman's coat. Dr Botherby at first gave him a long and confusing speech, but when Mr Jury did not accept this, he graciously conceded. At any rate, he thought, he had achieved his aim in making Mr Mond aware that if he could not do his job, he, Dr Botherby, was quite willing to do it for him.

Mr Jury returned triumphantly to the rehearsal and announced, 'Veni, vidi, vici - I came, I saw, I conquered!'

'Well done, sir,' said Ernest sincerely. 'Right, I don't think we need to go through Act Two, but we really must look at Act Three, especially from a logistical point of view. Remember, when the curtain comes down, the two footmen and I will change the scene to the countess' boudoir.'

They practised this manoeuvre very successfully, then began Act Three. Rupert, dressed as the page, timidly entered the boudoir and gave a message to the Countess. Quivering with a passion so compelling that nobody would have known it was feigned, he poured out his love for her most eloquently. She listened to him with cold composure, as he gazed at her adoringly, or rather, not at her, but at a glorious image in his mind. She began to reply, softened now towards him. Suddenly, her husband called to her offstage.

'Ernest, I can't possibly get under that bed,' declared Rupert, breaking the atmosphere.

'Are you sure? Couldn't you just hold your stomach in?'

Rupert looked at him haughtily, 'It has nothing to do with my stomach. The issue is not that I am too fat but that the bed is too low. You will see what I mean if you try getting under it yourself.'

'That's fine, I will take your word for it,' replied Ernest hastily, feeling that to attempt it would not contribute to his dignity. 'Mr Jury, is it possible to find another bed?'

'No,' the Latin teacher shook his head gravely.

'I have an idea,' said Rupert. 'If I hide on top of the bed instead, she can throw a heap of blankets and cushions on top of me before the Count enters; this is what happens to Don Juan in Canto I of Byron's poem, and he would have escaped detection had he not left his shoes beside the bed.'

'Excellent! Mr Mond will like that, I think, especially if we explain the reference to him,' said Ernest happily. 'Anyhow, Mrs Johnson cut the scene out entirely on grounds of it being inappropriate, so I don't think it matters how we do it. Carry on! Oh, by the way, try not to suffocate him with the blankets.'

The performance that afternoon was a great success. As Ernest had predicted, Mr Mond was delighted with the interpretation, particularly of those scenes which had been cut by Mrs Johnson. Even the steam train scene worked smoothly, as Mr Jury, fired by his victory over Dr Botherby, exerted himself to defeat the projector.

'Hello, did you enjoy my play? Rupert was very good, I thought, though I would never have thought of casting him for a womanising role. Obviously, Ernest knows him better, eh?' Mr Mond remarked jovially to Rupert's parents afterwards.

'Thank you, I enjoyed the play very much. It was

very original and unique,' Rupert's mother smiled flatteringly.

'Indeed, it's the funniest play I've seen in a long time,' chimed in his father, before Rupert could stop him. 'Absolutely hilarious, in fact. Have a nice half term!'

Mr Mond was much gratified by these comments, though a little perplexed by that of Rupert's father, for the play was meant to be a tragedy. Perhaps, he reflected, I really am a great playwright, for the audience appears to be discovering hidden meanings which I had not thought of myself. The learned Dr Botherby himself could not have done better.

Being in an unusually sociable mood, Rupert's father suggested to Ada, Beatrice and Bertie that they accompany them to a tea shop on the High Street. As this proposition met with enthusiasm from the children and no objections even from Bertie's Aunt Caroline, they all trooped off to the aforesaid tea shop. A pleasant scent rose from a china teapot, and an array of cakes completed everybody's feeling of profound contentment at the end of term.

'I thought you were both brilliant today,' Ada remarked warmly to the boys. 'I particularly enjoyed the scene in which Rupert seduced the Countess. I really don't know how you managed to act being in love so well.'

'Perhaps because I know something about it in real life,' he smiled. 'I'm not as silly and childish as you think, you know.'

'What I should like to know,' mused Bertie, 'is how

you guessed the truth about Mr Beanacre, Rupert.'

'Well, I actually had the epiphany when we were sitting in the common room of St Cecelia's house, and I happened to overhear someone talking about Mr Mond's play. Mr Mond, you see, lives next door to Mr Beanacre, by the Cathedral. Once I considered the possibility that the man who visited Miss Gourlay was not the man who was observing our investigations, the solution became obvious. This man must have been in close proximity to Mr Mond in order to influence his mind as he wrote the play. He must also be within the school in order to suppress Margaret. Therefore, he must be a member of staff who does not board, but lives in the village. He must also be intimate with Miss Gourlay, and the whole school remarked upon the untypical friendliness of Mr Beanacre towards her. Finally, he must be a powerful wizard, and at that moment, I suddenly remembered what Mama had said some weeks ago about him not being an ordinary human. All these factors pointed me towards Mr Beanacre. Incidentally, on the timetables, it says Mr J. Beanacre: presumably the initial stands for Julius,' explained Rupert. 'Of course, I did not realise that he was her father. That came as a great shock.'

'That was brilliant, how you deduced that,' said Bertie admiringly.

'Oh, it was elementary, my dear Watson,' he laughed.

Ada said, 'So now the mystery is solved, except for one small detail. How did the Bursar of Urganda College see through your disguise?'

'I've thought about this,' replied Rupert, 'and this is what I think: when the Bursar called for champagne, he still did not suspect, but he must have caught sight of the ring, which was still on my finger, as I poured him a glass. The family arms would have been familiar to him, you see. Well, I know now to be careful about that in future.'

'If we have any more adventures like this,' put in Beatrice.

'Ah, but adventures have a habit of continuing once they begin, in my experience,' said Rupert's father.

'Indeed, and in the future, I shan't rely on Papa appearing as a deus ex machina to save me.'

'What a shame! I rather like being a deus ex machina. It is good for my ego,' he smiled. 'Ah, Bertie, I can see your Aunt Caroline and your mother approaching, so it seems to be time to break up our merry party. Have a pleasant holiday!'

As they got up to go, Ada asked Rupert, 'What do you intend to do in the holidays?'

'Not much,' he replied. 'I shall study, though.'

'Study? Is that necessary?' cried Bertie. 'After all, you did get over ninety per cent in all the tests this term.'

'I meant studying magic, actually,' he explained. 'Well, see you all next term. And now, Papa, you must admit that Mr Mond was in fact a great playwright of the 21st Century.'

'Well, that's not saying much, is it?' he replied, fondly ruffling his son's wavy dark hair, as they rounded the bend at the Cathedral and gazed back at

St Jude's, before vanishing into the air.

BOOKS BY THIS AUTHOR

Claude And The Dark Force

St Jude's Cathedral School And The Oxford League Of Witches

St Jude's Cathedral School And The Paper People

Printed in Great Britain
by Amazon